FROZEN
TEARS

NOVELS FOR ADULT LEARNERS

FROZEN TEARS

DON SAWYER

CENTRE FOR CURRICULUM, TRANSFER AND TECHNOLOGY

VICTORIA, BRITISH COLUMBIA

FROZEN TEARS
by Don Sawyer
Copyright © 1997 by the Province of British Columbia
Ministry of Education, Skills and Training
All rights reserved.

This novel has been written especially for adults learners improving their reading skills. The development and production was funded by the Province of British Columbia, Ministry of Education, Skills and Training and Human Resources Development Canada, National Literacy Secretariat.

Project coordination: Centre for Curriculum, Transfer and Technology
Design and production coordination: Bendall Books
Cover design and illustration: Bernadette Boyle

CANADIAN CATALOGUING IN PUBLICATION DATA
Sawyer, Don.
    Frozen Tears
    (Novels for adult learners)
    ISBN 0-7718-9491-0
    1. High interest-low vocabulary books. 2. Readers
(Adult) I. Centre for Curriculum, Transfer and
Technology. II. Title. III. Series.
    PS8587.A3F76 1997   428'.62   C97-960065-0
    PR9199.3S3F76 1997

ORDER COPIES FROM
Marketing Department
Open Learning Agency
4355 Mathissi Place
Burnaby, BC, Canada V5G 4S8
Telephone: 604-431-3210
Toll-free: 1-800-663-1653
Fax: 604-431-3381
Order Number: VA0192

CONTACT FOR INFORMATION
Centre for Curriculum, Transfer and
Technology
5th Floor, 1483 Douglas Street
Victoria, BC, Canada V8W 3K4
Telephone: 250-387-6065
Fax: 250-387-9142

ALSO IN THE SERIES, NOVELS FOR ADULT LEARNERS
THE BUCKLE by Don Sawyer
CROCODILES AND RIVERS by Don Sawyer
THE MAILBOX by Kate Ferris
THE SCOWLING FROG by Kate Ferris
THREE WISE MEN by Kate Ferris

ACKNOWLEDGEMENTS

While this is a work of fiction, the author is deeply indebted to Diane Burk for sharing her experiences and contributing significantly to the writing of this book. I would also like to thank Kim MacMillan, Rainer Abramzik and Reg Walters for their technical advice.

1

Laura looked at the clock. Ten to three. Only 10 more minutes until school got out. Mr. Patterson, her seventh grade teacher, droned on at the front of the classroom. Most of the other kids doodled or shuffled papers. Allison and Scott passed notes. Paul seemed asleep on his desk. Laura stared out the window.

Outside it was already beginning to get dark. The leafless trees were black and brittle. White hills rolled toward the darkening sky. It was cold. The coldest day of the winter. Probably minus 30 already, Laura figured. It was going to be a bitterly cold night. At home the horses would be standing in a circle in their corrals. Great clouds of steam would be puffing from their nostrils.

Home. Or what there was of it. She felt the sting in her cheek where her father had slapped her that morning with his open hand. Laura had spilled milk while pouring it on her corn flakes.

"George!" her mother had shrilled. "Did you see what she did?"

Her father looked up. His small eyes blazed. He lunged over the table and his huge hand crashed into the side of her face. Her head had snapped around sharply. Tears sprang to her eyes. But she would not cry. Her two younger sisters said nothing. They stared silently at the table.

The mark of her father's hand was burned into her cheek. On the bus, other kids saw it but said nothing. It wasn't the first time. In school, teachers didn't give her a second glance. They had seen it before too.

Laura remembered the endless beatings. They had gone on as long as she could remember. Not every day, but almost. Laura thought about the strap her father had carefully carved from a leather thresher belt. And the bullwhip he hung on a nail inside the front door. She heard it crack around her legs. She heard herself screaming.

"Miss Martin, do you have something you'd like to share with the class?"

Students' faces were staring at her. Oh, Christ, thought Laura. What have I done?

The teacher stalked down the aisle toward Laura's desk. "What was the meaning of that outburst?"

Laura felt fear begin to rise in her chest. Then it turned to something else. Anger. Hatred.

He was over her now. He peered at her through black-framed glasses. He was tall with thinning brown hair. It was brushed back and held in place with some sort of oil. His lips were pressed tightly together.

"Did you hear me, young lady? I asked you…"

Laura exploded out of the desk before he could finish. She leapt at him, the anger igniting inside her. She dug her nails into the thin face staring at her. She saw him lurch back, terror on his face. His glasses flew off. They skittered along the wood floor.

Now her hands were on his chest, pushing, pounding. Mr. Patterson squealed. He shoved her sharply on the shoulders. She fell back and sat heavily on the floor. The teacher scrambled back down the aisle. He dashed to the door.

At the door he turned. "This is far from over, young lady! I'll be back with the principal. I'm sure your father will be interested in hearing about this!"

Then he was gone. The room was perfectly silent. Tears stung Laura's eyes, but she did not cry. What should she do? This time they would kick her out of school for a month. She thought back to the last time she had been suspended. She had never seen her father so enraged. He had dragged her out to the barn. He had beaten her with the whip until her legs were bleeding from deep red welts. Then he grabbed some barbed wire. He twisted it into a noose. He jammed it over her head.

"I'll hang you," he had hissed. "I swear I will."

Laura still felt the barbs dig into her neck. Felt the sickening fear. If her father hadn't noticed Laura's mother in the door Laura wondered if he would have done it.

What would he do now?

Laura stood up. Rows of silent faces stared at her. She walked to the door and looked down the hall. No one was there. She rushed to her locker and pulled her sweater out. It was knit out of thick brown and white wool. She zipped it up. Then she wrapped her scarf around her neck. She pulled off her runners and yanked on her low brown rubber boots. They were trimmed in fake black fur. Laura grabbed the thin wool gloves from the top shelf. She thrust her hands inside. She heard loud voices at the end of the hall. She left her locker door open and ran to the nearest exit.

Opening the door was like walking into a freezer. The cold bit into her face. She turned the collar up on her sweater. It was totally dark now. And she was alone. In the driveway in front of the school she saw the school bus. Its lights were on. Laura knew it would be warm inside. For a moment she was tempted to board the bus. Take her chances with her father. Then she thought about the barbed wire noose.

But if she didn't go home, where could she go? She didn't know anyone in town. She didn't even know where her few friends lived.

Except for Sarah. Laura knew Sarah's mother, Rachel, a little. She had met her at rodeos and at horse auctions. Laura had seen the way Rachel stared at her father with cold eyes. And she remembered the time her father had slapped her at the Clinton rodeo. Rachel had gripped Sarah's hand hard. She had glared at Laura's father with disgust. Her father was about to smack Laura again. Then he saw Rachel's stare and dropped his hand. "Bitch," he muttered. "Mind your own business." But he had stalked away. And he left Laura alone for the rest of the day.

Laura knew Rachel and Sarah lived off the highway at 49 mile. North. But the highway was miles away. Besides, they'd be looking for her there. Her only chance was to go overland. But how far was it… 20, 25 miles? How would she find it? With luck she'd hit the side road that ran from the highway toward the river. But that would be hours. In the dark.

She heard shouting inside the school. Laura looked through the glass in the orange door. Inside the principal was standing with Mr. Patterson. They were pointing to the outside door. The principal began walking toward it quickly. Laura glanced at the dim white hills in front of her. She pulled her scarf around her neck and waded into the snow. She headed north.

2

It had been three hours since Laura had left the school. The cold gnawed at her feet. They felt heavy and numb, like cement. At least the pain had gone away. She couldn't feel her fingers on her cheeks. Her ears burned like they were on fire.

In the darkness she saw another fence ahead of her. She pushed through the knee-high snow and leaned against the barbed wire strands. She was so tired. She just wanted to sleep. It had begun to snow. A light dusting powdered her sweater and hair. How much farther to the road? Another 10 miles? More? She didn't know. Barely cared.

At last she pushed the top strand upward. Clumsily she crawled between the wires. She felt the barbs catch on her sweater. She tried to unsnag them with her frozen fingers. Finally she fell into the snow on the other side. She rolled down a ditch. She felt the snow burn her bare wrists. Laura pulled herself to her knees. Was there a road at the top of the ditch? She struggled up the side. At the top she could make out faint tracks in the deep snow. It was a road of some sort. Could it be the road to Sarah's?

Couldn't be. That would be miles north yet. Besides, that would be a major road. This was little more than a track. Should she follow it? She looked to her left. There seemed to be a dull glow behind a clump of trees 100 metres away. It was too bright for a house. Laura stumbled along the packed ruts toward the glow. She was grateful not to be fighting deep snow.

As she neared the trees the glow got brighter. She rounded a bend and realized she was in the yard of a small saw mill. Trees were piled in a dark heap. The moon glinted dully off a large round blade under a low roof. And a few metres away a huge pile of slab wood burned. Even from where she stood Laura could feel the heat. She rushed toward the glowing pile.

It had been burning for several hours. The pile of scrap had probably originally been 10 feet high. Now it had settled to about four or five feet. Sparks and smoke rose into the darkness. They twisted together and disappeared into the night. The burning wood glowed like blood. Laura felt the wave of heat as she limped into the ring of light around the pile. The ground was wet under her feet where the fire had melted the snow. She felt the heat sear her frozen face. She stood as close as she could. She was exhausted. Steam began to rise off her wet sweater. She felt it scorching her arm. But she didn't care. She was warm.

Laura slumped to the ground. Her feet underneath her still felt numb. She knew they must be frozen. Her back felt the chill of the bitterly cold night behind her. Her eyelids began to close. She lay back on the coarse wet grass. She fell into an uneasy sleep.

Laura awoke as the earliest hints of day lightened the eastern sky. The pile had shifted with a soft roar. A tower of sparks rose into the sky. Her toes and fingers ached like they were in a vice. Her face burned. Her arms felt raw and inflamed from the steam. She sat up. She figured it was six or seven. Laura didn't want to be there when the mill workers came.

Standing took great effort. Moving beyond the narrow strip of warmth was the hardest thing she had ever done. The cold bit into her again like sharp teeth. She tottered back down the track. Soon she saw her footprints where she had crossed the ditch. They were partially filled with last night's snow. She trudged across the road and into the field beyond. She headed north again.

The next two hours were a blur of agony and pain. Her thawed toes and fingers froze again. She had wrapped the scarf around her face. Now it was heavy with ice from her frozen breath. The snow dragged at her. She plodded on.

The morning had turned the sky from black to grey. The world was painted in shades of grey and white. She walked more and more slowly. Her eyelashes froze to her face. She didn't notice.

Suddenly she ran into a long snow bank. It was frozen hard. It was not high, but Laura could hardly get over it. She crawled to the top and rolled down the other side. When she got up she realized she was on a plowed road. She knew it was Sarah's road. She was too tired to feel much joy. Just relief.

She looked left. Then right. Which way? How far was she along the road? Was she past Sarah's farm? She knew the wrong decision would cost her life. She knew she could not go much farther.

Sarah lived near the river. Laura knew that. She had not seen the river all night. It must still be to the west. She turned wearily to the left. She toiled slowly down the road.

Laura heard the dogs before she saw the gate. They were clustered near the road barking hoarsely. A bright red mailbox stood on a wood post. Laura stared at it. "Thomas" was written on the side. She smiled. She wanted to cry. But she couldn't. All her tears were frozen somewhere inside her. She turned and walked down the drive.

Rachel heard the dogs. She looked up and peered out the kitchen window. Sarah was eating oatmeal at the round table near the wood stove.

"Oh, my God," Rachel whispered. "It's Laura."

"Laura? Are you sure?"

But Rachel was already out the door. She was wearing only slippers and a thin robe. The morning was still brutally cold. But Rachel didn't feel it. Laura was staggering down the plowed drive. Rachel rushed to her.

Rachel put her arm around the girl's shuddering shoulders. "Oh, my God," she whispered again.

Ice hung from Laura's dark hair. Her ears were white and cracked. Her skin over her high cheekbones was white as ice. Here eyelashes were frozen. She limped painfully.

"Sarah told me what happened. How did you get here?"

Laura could hardly speak. Her tongue felt thick. "Walked," she finally managed.

"You walked? All night?"

Laura just nodded.

"Please," she mumbled. "May I come inside?"

Rachel helped Laura up the stairs onto the back porch. Sarah stared out the window in horror.

"No. Not yet."

Laura nearly wept. "Please," she begged. "Please just let me warm up in the house."

"If I do," Rachel said softly, "you'll lose your toes. Your ears. Maybe your fingers. Wait here. Just a minute."

Laura was too exhausted to argue. She leaned against the door frame.

Rachel reappeared. She carried a metal tub. In the other hand she had a can of coal oil, which was used to treat frostbite. She sat Laura on a chair. She poured coal oil into the tub. Then she carefully pulled the thin rubber boots off Laura's feet. She gently peeled the frozen socks off. Laura could hardly feel her. Rachel placed Laura's feet in the oil. Then she helped Laura off with her gloves. She wiped the frozen fingers with oil. Then she took off Laura's sweater, stiff with ice. She pulled off her shirt and bathed her raw arms.

Soon Laura was almost naked on the porch. She just wanted to pass out. She was vaguely aware of Sarah's mother bathing her. She could feel the rag slide over her. She smelled the reek of the oil. She heard Rachel crying quietly.

It seemed to take hours. Finally Rachel wrapped Laura in an old quilt. She helped her into the kitchen. The heat was almost unbearable. Laura sat numbly on a chair. Sarah had drawn a cool bath. Now Rachel helped Laura into the bathroom. She took off the last of Laura's clothes and guided her into the tub.

The water felt like liquid fire. Pain jolted from her feet and fingers. Her ears were aflame. She cried out. Then she settled into the water. Rachel washed her gently. Laura began to doze off.

Rachel and Sarah helped Laura out of the tub. Rachel slipped a flannel nightgown over Laura's head. Sarah took one arm and Rachel the other. Together they carried her up a flight of stairs to a bedroom. Laura crawled under the covers and lay on her back. Rachel pulled the quilt up to Laura's chin. Laura started to swim into sleep. But just before she did she felt Rachel bend over her. She kissed Laura on her forehead.

Sarah burst through the door. "Mom! There's a black pickup pulling into the driveway! I think it's Laura's dad!"

Laura was sitting in front of the wood stove. A wave of fear rose from her stomach. She felt like she was going to faint.

It had been a week since she had staggered into Sarah's farm. Her ears were still oozing, despite the Watkins Cobalt Salve Rachel put on them morning and night. The skin over her cheekbone was black and cracked. Her toes had turned dark. But Rachel was sure Laura wouldn't lose them.

Laura was beginning to feel safe. Loved, maybe for the first time in her life. Now her father had come for her.

Rachel grabbed her fringed leather jacket from a peg beside the door. She hesitated. Then she turned to a gun rack by the basement door. She walked over and took down a deer rifle. She quickly slipped two shells into the magazine.

"Stay inside," she ordered. "No matter what happens, stay inside. Both of you."

The storm door slammed shut. Sarah and Laura watched as Rachel approached the truck that had just rolled to a stop. When her father got out, Laura felt the rush of nausea again. She knew she was going to faint. Then Sarah silently put her arm around Laura's shoulders. Laura felt better.

Laura's father was a big bear of a man. Thick black hair sprang out from under a black cowboy hat. A tangled black beard covered most of his face. He wore a greasy green vest over a red and black checked flannel shirt. He angrily slammed the truck door and swung around the front of the truck. Then he saw Rachel. He slowed. He saw the rifle across her arms. He stopped.

They couldn't hear everything. Mainly what Laura's father shouted: "I'm not leaving here without her. You hear? This is none of your damned business! Why, I should…"

When he started to advance, Rachel swung the gun up. She worked the bolt. Laura's father stopped again. Laura had seen the look in his eyes before. It was raw, violent rage.

Rachel lowered the rifle slightly. Now it pointed just slightly over Laura's father's head. Laura and Sarah heard Sarah's mother say something. Laura's father cursed. He started toward her again. Rachel dropped the end of the gun more. Laura's father was 10 metres away. The rifle was pointed directly at his chest.

He cursed some more. Then he turned abruptly toward the

truck. He kicked the bumper viciously. He turned back toward Rachel.

"This isn't the end of this!" he roared. "Far from it!" He got into his truck and slammed the door. He jammed the pickup into gear and let out the clutch. The tires spun on the packed snow. They whined as the truck fishtailed out the driveway.

Rachel dropped the barrel of the gun. She turned back to the house. She opened the door and walked inside. She carefully took the shells out of the rifle. Then she put it back on the rack. Sarah and Laura were still holding each other by the window.

"Thanks, Mrs. Thomas," Laura said quietly. "Thanks a lot."

Rachel hung her jacket back up on its peg. She sighed and stared out the kitchen door window.

"But he's right, you know," she said at last.

"How do you mean?" Laura asked.

"This *isn't* the end of it. He'll be back. Probably with the RCMP." She turned to the girls. "I guess we'll worry about that later, eh?"

Rachel tried to smile. But Laura noticed that there was no spark in her dark brown eyes.

3

It had been two weeks since her father had left the farm in a rage. Laura's frozen ears and cheeks were beginning to heal. And inside she was beginning to thaw too. At first Laura had been frightened. Scared that Sarah's mother would turn her into the police. Or worse, to her parents. Afraid that her father would come and yank her into his truck.

But slowly Laura had begun to feel safe. She just wanted to stay with Sarah and Rachel forever.

When the RCMP pulled into the drive, all the old fear came flooding back. She heard the tires on the cold gravel. from the kitchen window she saw the white car with the uniformed men inside. Rachel was already at the back door. She stared through the glass panes.

"Go into the living room," she said quietly. "Let me talk to them."

Laura ran into the next room. She huddled in a corner of the big green sofa. Laura heard a knock at the door.

"Mrs. Thomas?" a man's voice asked.

"Call me Rachel, Carl. You've known me for almost 10 years."

"Yes, well…" The constable cleared his throat nervously. "Mrs. Thomas, Rachel. We have a complaint from George Martin. He says you're holding his daughter."

Rachel snorted. "Protecting her is more like it. Carl, you know what goes on at that place. You know what a monster he is."

Laura heard the constable shift his feet uneasily. "That may be." His voice softened a little. "But I really don't have any choice. She has to come with us. There's a hearing in town this afternoon. The judge will decide where she goes."

There was a long silence. "And if I don't give her up?"

"Martin has threatened to lay charges of kidnapping. And we would have to charge you with obstruction." The constable cleared his throat again. "I'm sorry, Rachel."

"Can I come to the hearing?"

"No. Just the parents and the judge. They'll give her a chance to speak."

"Sure," Rachel replied bitterly. "A girl so terrified of her father that she faints from fear when she sees him. I'm sure she will be able to tell her side of the story very effectively."

"I'm sorry," the constable said again. "But that's the way it is."

There was another long silence. Laura heard the constables' feet scraping on the wood porch.

"Are you going to give her up?" the constable said at last. "Or do we have to come in and get her?"

Rachel was crying quietly. Laura stared blankly at the door into the kitchen. The two constables walked into the living room. They wore short, heavy coats. Both had guns strapped to their belts. Rachel leaned against the door frame. Her hand was over her mouth. She didn't look at Laura.

"Laura Martin?" It was the voice of the constable that had spoken with Rachel.

Laura looked up at the men. She couldn't say anything.

"Laura," the constable said more gently. "You have to come with us."

Laura felt numb. It was like she was frozen again. She stood up slowly on the carpeted floor. Outside the sky was low and grey.

"Get your coat."

Laura walked into the kitchen. She took her sweater off the peg. She put it on. Then she pulled on her low rubber boots. She felt nothing. The fear had given way to emptiness. A terrible emptiness.

The second constable opened the back door. Laura walked outside into the cold. The storm door slammed behind her. She followed the two men to their car. One of them opened the back door. She climbed inside. It was still warm. A metal screen separated her from the front. The two officers opened the front doors. They slid in. The first constable started the engine. He turned the car around. Laura looked back at the house. Rachel was standing outside the door. Tears welled from her eyes. She had only a thin flannel shirt on. Laura wondered if she was cold.

The police car moved quickly up the drive. And Rachel was gone.

"**M**iss Martin," the judge began. "Your parents say you are incorrigible. Do you know what that means?"

Laura sat alone at a small table. At the front of the room the judge sat behind a raised bench. Her parents sat at another table across from her. Neither had looked at her once. Laura stared at the judge. She said nothing.

"Incorrigible means that you are unmanageable. And that you cannot be reformed in a normal family setting. Do you understand now?"

Laura gave a slight nod.

The judge sighed. "Your parents have written this all out. You have quite a record." He pushed his glasses down his nose. Then he began to read from a typed paper. "Expelled from school five times. The last time you attacked a teacher. Failing marks since grade two. Constantly fighting with other students. Disrespectful of your parents. Rebellious."

The judge looked over the top of his glasses. "Young lady, what are we going to do with you?"

Laura glanced around the courtroom. The RCMP constable that had brought her in sat at a desk near the judge. A woman was taking notes beside him. Laura stared back at the judge. His black robes made him look like a giant crow.

The judge sighed again. "Your parents are not willing to take you back. And since you are 12 years old, I don't have much choice. I'm making you a ward of the court. And I'm sending you to Willingdon Detention Centre for the time being. Do you understand?"

Laura still stared numbly at the judge. She said nothing. She glanced quickly at her parents. They were already standing to leave. They had looks of satisfaction on their faces. They still did not look at her.

The judge looked disapprovingly at Laura's parents. They sat back down.

"Will you need time to pack, Laura?" the judge asked.

"Nah." It was her mother. It was the first time either of her parents had spoken. "We brought her stuff."

She pushed an old gym bag with her foot.

The judge looked over his glasses at Laura's mother. "Is that it?"

Her mother put her hands on her hips and glared at the judge. "Yeah. That's it. That's all she'll need."

The judge sat back. "All right. Constable Lucas, will you take Miss Martin? Put her in the detention room. Mrs. Johnson will be here shortly. We don't have a youth holding facility. You and Mrs. Johnson will have to take Miss Martin to Willingdon on tonight's train."

The officer stood up. He picked up the gym bag and walked to a door. Laura walked over to him. He led her out of the court room down a hall. He opened the door into a white room. A counter was at one end. Orange plastic chairs lined the walls. Laura sat down and stared out the one window. It was dark now. The low clouds blocked the moon.

The train trip to Burnaby took all night. Mrs. Johnson was a social worker. She was a large woman who wore an enormous dress. She didn't say much. She and the RCMP officer dozed in their seats. Laura sat and looked out the dark window. She had never been on a train. Where was it going? What was Willingdon? Was it a prison? What would happen to her? At least she was not being sent back home. Then she thought of Sarah and her mother. She thought about the soft quilt Rachel pulled up around Laura's neck when she tucked her in at night. Her throat swelled. But she did not cry. Her eyes closed. She slipped into an uneasy sleep.

They arrived at the train station early in the morning. An RCMP car was waiting for them. Mrs. Johnson sat in the back. The constable sat up front with another officer. As they drove, Laura peered out the side window. Laura had never been in a town larger than Williams Lake. She had never seen so many shops. Pizza restaurants, theaters, hardware stores, super markets lined the busy road. And there was no snow. A slow drizzle wet the sidewalks. The street lights glinted on the wet asphalt. Only the windshield wipers broke the silence.

They drove for a long time. Finally they pulled up in front of a tall wire gate. On each side of the gate high chain-link fences stretched for the entire block. They must have been at least 12 feet, Laura guessed. At the top, strands of barbed wire slanted inward.

A uniformed guard came out of a small building by the gate. He had a clipboard in his hands. He spoke quietly with the officer driving. Then he lifted a latch. He swung the gates inward. The car drove inside.

It was still dark. But bright streetlights lit up the area. Laura could see the fence enclosed a large grassy area. Maybe four or five blocks square. Inside, the drive led to a large three-storey building. Other smaller buildings were scattered around the grounds. It was quiet.

The car pulled up in front of the large building. Mrs. Johnson got out. The officer that had come down with her opened the back door for Laura. She got out and followed the officer inside. They walked up to a counter. A middle-aged woman in a blue uniform stood behind the counter. She looked sleepy. She was talking with Mrs. Johnson.

The RCMP officer slid some papers over the counter. The woman glanced at them. Then she looked at Laura. Laura stared silently back at her. The woman smiled.

"Well, Miss Martin, you must be tired. Let's get you to bed. We'll sort this paper work out tomorrow."

She lifted a hinged section of the counter. Laura walked through.

"Laura."

Laura turned around. It was the constable that had taken her from Sarah's.

He held his hat in his hands. "Good luck."

4

The next two weeks were a nightmare for Laura. She was kept separate from the other girls. She spent her nights in a small room with barred windows. Her days were spent in interviews and tests with long boring hours in between. The walls of her room were white. The walls of the clinic where they tested her were white. The uniforms worn by the nurses and doctors were white. The lights in the waiting room were harsh and white. She wore out the few comic books she could read. The only thing she looked forward to was the hour a day outside in the exercise yard. Laura saw other girls in blue jeans and white shirts. They were walking from building to building. Sometimes they would be playing basketball. But she was kept apart from them.

Nobody explained anything. Once she was ushered into an office. Before she sat down the man began reading questions from a paper in a file folder. How did she feel about her father? Had she ever considered suicide? Did she ever feel life was not worth living? He read the questions in a flat voice. Laura gave short answers. He wrote quick notes.

Then he closed the file. "You may go now," he said. He had never looked at her.

But the worst experience occurred three days after she had arrived. A nurse came and got her from the waiting room. Laura was leafing through a *Chatelaine* magazine looking at the pictures for the third time.

"Come with me," the nurse ordered.

Laura followed her into a white examination room. A metal table was pushed against one wall. A strip of white paper covered the table top. Two metal prongs stuck out of the end. Laura thought they looked a little like stirrups.

The nurse handed her a green gown. "Take your clothes off and put this on," she said.

"All of them?"

"Of course all of them," the woman snapped. "Just like you always do when you have a physical exam."

Laura had never seen a doctor. She had certainly never had a complete examination. She had never had her clothes off in front of another person.

Reluctantly she pulled off her jeans and unbuttoned her shirt. But she couldn't take off her panties. She just couldn't. She slipped on the gown. Maybe they wouldn't notice.

Half an hour later a man walked in. He had on a white coat and carried a clipboard.

"Up on the table," he ordered.

He looked in Laura's ears. Up her nose. He had her open her

mouth and studied her teeth and gums. He stuck a cold stethoscope against her bare back and had her cough.

"OK, put your feet in the stirrups."

Laura looked uncertainly at the metal prongs.

"Come on, come on. I don't have all day."

Hesitantly, Laura put one heel in the left stirrup. Then she put her other foot up.

"Well, lie down."

Laura lay down. The doctor pulled up her gown.

"What the hell?" he roared. "Get those pants off. Now!"

Laura yanked her legs back. She grabbed her knees and curled into a ball. If they wanted her panties off they'd have to take them off.

"Nurse!" the doctor roared. Two women entered the room. The doctor turned Laura over. One nurse held her legs down. The other grabbed her panties by the elastic. She began to pull.

Laura kicked and screamed. She twisted and squirmed. She heard the nylon rip. Then she was naked on the table. "Tie her," the doctor ordered.

One of the nurses wrapped rubber tubing around her wrists. She tied them to rings on the sides of the table. The other yanked her legs into the stirrups. She wrapped them tightly to the cold metal with more tubing. Laura was helpless.

Laura stared up at the white ceiling. She felt ice cold forceps being forced into her. She tried to shut out sound. Feelings.

Finally they were done. The nurses untied her.

"We'd better not have any more of that, young lady," the doctor said. "Or you'll find yourself in isolation." Laura kept staring at the ceiling. "Now get your clothes back on. The nurse will take you back to the waiting room."

The door closed. Laura was alone. She wanted to cry. No tears would come.

After two weeks the tests were done. A matron in a blue skirt and matching blue blouse found Laura sitting in her room. She was staring out the window across from her. Here it seemed to rain every day. Outside it was grey and colourless.

"Laura Martin?" the woman asked from the door.

Laura turned and looked at her silently.

"Would you bring your bag please. I will be taking you to your cottage."

Wordlessly, Laura stood up. She picked up her bag and followed the woman. They walked outside in the cold rain. The woman led her to a one-storey white building. A row of barred windows lined the outside. A metal sign said "Bungalow 2."

The matron pushed open the front door. Laura walked inside. There was an office on the right. Through a large window Laura saw a woman in a blue outfit similar to the matron's. She was typing at a desk. The woman was plump and had short black hair. There were lines around her eyes, like she smiled a lot.

On the left there was a large room. Sofas and upholstered chairs were arranged in a semicircle. A big television sat on a high metal stand. A long hallway extended in front of Laura. Another stretched to her left. The hallways were lined with doors.

A few girls walked by. They barely glanced at Laura.

The matron that had brought her over knocked on the office door. The black-haired woman looked up from the typewriter. She stood up and walked to the door and opened it.

"Hello, Carol. Who do we have here?" She smiled at Laura. The lines around her eyes crinkled.

"Laura Martin," the matron said, handing over a file. "She's gone through observation. She's assigned to your cottage."

The smiling woman stuck out her hand. Laura took it uncertainly. "I'm Martha Blackmore," she said. "The girls call me Blackie. I'm your housemother."

Laura said nothing and nodded.

"Not too talkative, eh?" the woman smiled. "Well, that's OK. After what they put you through in observation I don't blame you. Come on, let me take you to your room."

Blackie led Laura down the hall in front of her. Halfway down she stopped in front of a doorway on her right. A number "6" was screwed on the heavy wood door.

"This is it, Laura. We have 20 girls here. Each with her own room." She opened the door with a key on a ring around her wrist. Laura looked inside. To her right there was a bed with a bright red quilt on it. It had a lacy fringe around the edge. A white toilet was in the far corner. The sun had appeared outside. Sunlight streamed through a large window in front of her. The room was bright. White curtains almost hid the bars on the windows. A wooden desk and chair were pushed underneath the window. A small dresser was against the wall on her left.

"Why don't you get settled in? The girls have free time at five o'clock. Dinner's at six. Come down to the common room when you feel like it. Watch some TV."

Laura walked into the room. Blackie closed the door gently. Laura opened the old gym bag. She took out the few clothes inside. Then she put them in the chest of drawers. They barely filled one drawer. She emptied the bag out on the bed. A few hair bands, a brush and a comb fell out. Then a brown teddy bear tumbled onto the red bed cover. She picked it up. It was an old bear she'd been given by her grandmother before she'd died. How many years ago? It had a stitched smile on its furry face. It was soft. She sat down on the bed. She hugged the bear to her chest.

When Laura walked into the common room she was the only girl there. The television was on. Bugs Bunny was whacking Elmer Fudd with a frying pan. Laura sat down on a brown stuffed chair in front of the TV. She'd seen TV at her friends' houses. But they had never had one at home. She stared in fascination.

Other girls drifted into the room. None of them said anything to Laura. They barely seemed to notice her. Suddenly she was aware of someone standing over her. Laura looked up. A tall girl with short blond hair was scowling down at her.

"You're in my chair," she said curtly. "Get up. Now."

Laura looked around. All the chairs were full. She looked back at the TV.

"I said move!" the girl screamed. She grabbed Laura by the shoulders. She tried to yank her out of the chair.

Laura exploded. She wasn't good at a lot of things. But fighting was something she knew. She wasn't big. But years of working on the farm had made her strong. And years of scrapping at school and at home had made her tough.

When she came out of the chair she jammed her shoulder into the taller girl's stomach. Laura heard the girl groan. She fell back. Laura attacked. She threw a punch that landed hard on the girl's cheek. The girl tripped and sprawled on the floor. Laura threw herself on top. The girl grabbed Laura by her hair. She yanked her head down. Laura began punching the girl wildly in the face.

"What's going on here?" Blackie's voice was sharp, commanding. Laura felt the girl underneath her loosen her grip on Laura's hair. Laura stopped punching. She looked up. Blackie was standing over them. Her hands were on her large hips. She was not smiling.

"Stand up. Both of you."

Laura got to her feet. The other girl stood up. She tried to tuck her shirt into her jeans. Laura noticed with satisfaction that a thin trickle of blood flowed from her nose.

"Like I said, what's going on here?"

"She took my chair," the taller girl mumbled.

"What's that?"

"She took my chair," the girl said more loudly.

"Debbie, we don't have assigned chairs." The taller girl stared at the floor. "Do you understand that?"

The other girl said nothing. Blackie turned to Laura. "As for you, this is not a great start."

Laura stared at her defiantly. Blackie sounded angry. But there was something not quite right. Maybe it was a twinkle in her eye.

"Now I'm going to tell you both this once. If this happens again you'll find yourself in isolation."

"Aw, shove it, you old bitch," Debbie mumbled.

The other girls were watching. Laura had to show them she was tough too. "Yeah," she said. "Blow it out your ear."

Blackie laughed out loud. "What was that?"

Laura was embarrassed. "I said, 'Blow it out your ear,'" she repeated more quietly.

Blackie's eyes were crinkled in a smile. "That's one of the nicest things anyone's said to me in here." She laughed again. "After what I've been called, that's downright sweet."

She clapped her hands. "OK, that's enough. Let's get to dinner."

Debbie eyed Laura coldly and turned away. The other girls filed down the other hall. Laura followed them.

The corridor opened into a large dining room. Two long tables were in the middle. Blackie sat at the end of one. A cook stood behind a stainless steel table. She dished out food as the girls walked by with trays. Laura got in line. Then she sat down at one of the tables. She began eating. She listened to the other girls. They swore more than anyone she'd ever heard. Even more than her father.

The girl next to her jabbed Laura in the ribs. "Hey, what are you in here for?"

Laura looked at the girl. She was smaller than Laura. She had red hair. It was pulled back in a pony tail.

"I don't know," Laura replied. "Maybe slugging a teacher."

The other girl nodded. "After the way you took Debbie out, I can see that."

"How about you?" Laura asked.

"How about me what?"

"What are you in for?"

"Oh. Prostitution."

Laura chewed her food more slowly. "You mean having, uh, sex. With men. For money?"

The girl gave a short laugh. "Yeah. That's about the size of it."

"How old are you?"

"Fourteen."

Laura was silent.

"Say, how did you lose your cherry?" the other girl asked.

Laura stared at her tray blankly. "Uh, I didn't have any cherries. I had peaches."

The girl looked at her in disbelief for a moment. Then she exploded into laughter.

"Whoa!" she shouted. The other girls quieted. "Wait'll you hear this! I asked this chick how she lost her cherry. You know what she says? She says she didn't have cherries. She had peaches!"

Both tables erupted in hysterics. Laura slumped in her chair. She peered down at her plate. She had said something really dumb. But what was it?

After dinner, Laura walked back up the hall. Blackie came up behind her. She was walking with Carol, the woman who had brought Laura over earlier.

"Laura, can I see you a minute?" She walked to her office door and opened it. Laura went in. She sat on a green chair. Blackie sat behind her desk.

"I heard the girls laughing at you," she began gently. "Do you know what was so funny?"

Laura looked at her hands in her lap. She shook her head slightly.

"Cherry is a slang term for virginity. Ricki was asking you how you lost your virginity."

Laura felt her face turn red.

Blackie sat back in her chair. She sighed. "I'm sorry this has been such a hard day. It'll get easier. I promise."

Laura looked up into Blackie's plump face. She was smiling.

"Thanks," Laura said. She got up and went out the door. She leaned against the wall. Carol went inside. She left the door open. Laura could hear them speaking.

"You know, Carol. I don't believe that girl belongs here. She's a strong girl. Strong in will and strong physically."

"Yeah. I understand Debbie found that out today. Couldn't have happened to a nicer little bully."

Laura stood outside the door. She pressed against the wall.

"I've been at this a long time," Blackie went on. "I can feel it. She's a strong girl. But she's not a bad girl."

Laura felt her heart beat more quickly. She slid away from the door and walked toward her room. She sat down on her bed and picked up her teddy. She held it up and looked it in the face.

"Teddy," she whispered. "I'm not a bad girl." She hugged her bear and lay down on the covers.

5

The months settled into a routine for Laura. After breakfast she would go to school. Or what passed for school. Poor old Mrs. Brighouse. She tried, Laura could see. But the class was chaos. No one paid any attention. There would be fights in the back of the room. Loud conversations. Girls would stand up and walk over to the windows.

"Now, Donna," Mrs. Brighouse would admonish in her thin, wavering voice. "Please sit down. It's your turn to read from *Little House on the Prairie*."

Usually the girl identified would shout back some obscenity. Mrs. Brighouse would just sigh. "Well, Ricki, will you read?"

Ricki would snap her book shut. Maybe prop her feet up on the desk beside her. The girl in that desk would slap Ricki's feet off. "Get your god damned feet off of me!" And then Ricki would kick the desk. And the other girl would take a swing at Ricki. Other girls would start yelling.

So it went. Day after day. Laura kept to herself in the back of the room. Mrs. Brighouse was so busy with the general bedlam she generally ignored Laura. The teacher expected nothing from Laura. And Laura gave her nothing.

After school, Laura went to one of the vocational buildings. Some girls were taught hair dressing. But after two weeks of ruining girls' hair, Laura knew she'd never be a hairdresser. Blackie put her in sewing. And Laura found that she was pretty good at it. She learned to use a machine. To work from patterns. All the girls had to make their own white blouses. Laura's were always the best. And she loved to put little touches on them. A tiny flower embroidered in white on a collar. Her initials on a pocket. Something to set her apart. To make her special.

Then later in the afternoon there were sports. Laura was astonished one day to be given a swim suit. They were led to a beautiful pool next to the gym. Laura had never seen a pool.

"OK, girls," Mrs. Osborne ordered. She was their gym teacher. "Into the water."

The girls cursed and grumbled, but they reluctantly slid into the water. Except Laura.

"Laura!" Mrs. Osborne barked. "Into the water!"

Laura's mouth was set stubbornly. She stood on the cold tiles. Girls in the water splashed her. They whooped and hollered. "Chicken!" Laura folded her arms across her chest.

Mrs. Osborne walked over to her. "What's wrong?"

"I can't swim," Laura said quietly. "I'm afraid of the water."

"Well," Mrs. Osborne said, putting her arm across Laura's shoulders. "This is a good time to get over it." Suddenly she pushed Laura. Laura lost her balance. Arms waving, she sprawled into the water face first. She came up spluttering. She flailed the water in a panic. She gasped for air.

Mrs. Osborne stood smiling on the deck. "Put your feet down," she called. Laura stopped kicking. She put her feet down. They hit bottom. She stood up. She was in about three feet of water.

Ricki was in hysterics. Laura grabbed her by her red pony tail. She thought about drowning the little redhead. But Mrs. Osborne was not Mrs. Brighouse.

"Shut up, all of you!" Her voice boomed and echoed in the high-ceilinged pool. "Laura, let go of Ricki's hair. Now!"

Reluctantly Laura let go.

"This is swimming. Not wrestling. Let's get to it."

Laura was never very good. But she did get over her terror of the water. And she learned to swim.

She was also the star of the basketball court. She had a deadly outside shot. And she gained the respect of the older girls with her hard, aggressive play.

Before dinner she sat with the other girls and watched TV. She sat wherever she wanted to. No one argued with her again about chairs. After dinner the girls had free time. They could visit each other's room. But they could not close the doors.

Laura became friends with many of the girls. But though she liked them, their stories often shocked her. Their young lives were filled with sexual abuse. Drugs. Prostitution. Living on the streets. Most of them were city girls. They had seen and done things Laura never dreamed of. She was shaken by their lives. And horrified by the bleak futures they saw for themselves. Most had no hopes of escaping the cycle of drugs, prostitution and crime. No hopes period.

Over and over she saw girls leave. And weeks, maybe months later, they were back. More bruised. Coming down from drugs. More beaten and bitter.

A conviction developed inside her. At first it was hazy, unformed. But slowly it became clearer. Definite. Certain. She didn't know what she wanted. That wasn't it. But she knew with absolute clarity she did not want to go where these girls were headed. She did not want to become like them. She made a decision. She would follow another path.

Her conviction was reinforced by her work in the hospital. Each girl worked somewhere in the centre. Some worked on the grounds. Others cleaned. But the matrons and nurses soon learned that Laura had a special skill. She could work with new girls coming down from drugs.

When girls were first admitted, many had been doing drugs for months. Years. Some were addicted to alcohol. They were cleaned up in the detox unit. Laura was assigned there. Her job was to monitor the girls for a four-hour shift through a window that looked into the detox cell.

It was like a TV screen on hell. Especially when the girls were heroin addicts. She watched as the girls screamed, ranted and threw their bedding around the room. She cleaned them up when they had diarrhea. When they vomited. She called the nurses when they pulled their hair out in clumps, leaving bloody patches on their scalps. She helped restrain the girls when they smashed their heads against the wall. Took their spoon away when they gouged their wrists with its blunt edge.

Sometimes she tried to talk to them. To soothe their terrible craving. They cried and sobbed. Laura was patient. Steady. Trusted. One of them. But not one of them. She became respected by the staff and girls alike.

Six months after she had arrived at Willingdon, Blackie called Laura into her office. In that time she had not had a visitor. She had received a few letters from Rachel. That was all.

"Laura," Blackie began. "You've earned some weekends out." Laura knew that girls got points for good behaviour. They used them to visit outside of the centre. Usually with family.

Laura shrugged. "I've got no place to go."

"I know," Blackie said softly. "That's why I wondered if you would like to come with me. To be with my family some weekends."

Laura looked up. Blackie was leaning across her desk. The lines around her eyes crinkled.

"I, I don't know what to say. I don't want to be a burden," Laura said.

Blackie looked serious. But her eyes still twinkled.

"I wouldn't have asked you if I didn't mean it. We'll be disappointed if you don't visit us. What do you say?"

Laura smiled and shrugged again. "Sure. It would be great to get out sometimes."

"Good," Blackie smiled. "It's settled then. How about this weekend?"

Those weekends with Blackie's family became the centre of Laura's life. It wasn't just the places they took her. The exposure to ideas and places. It was also seeing a family that worked. A family that cared for one another. A family that ran on love. It was a chance to learn how a family should work.

Blackie and her husband, Tom, had two kids. Justin and Annie. Justin was six and Annie was eight. At first, Laura was quiet, withdrawn. But even from the beginning the children welcomed her. They chattered about their school. Annie showed Laura her hockey card collection. Justin introduced Laura to all his stuffed bears. And over the months Laura became more relaxed. She smiled more, talked more. She shared more of herself. And she watched.

One morning at breakfast during one of Laura's first visits, Justin and Annie got into a fight. Annie ate the last piece of bacon. Justin started to cry.

"Justin, you're such a baby," Annie taunted.

"Am not!" Justin cried.

"You are too!" Annie yelled back.

"That's enough, Annie," Blackie broke in. "Let's see how we can settle this. Annie, is Justin a baby?"

Annie twisted her mouth. "No. I guess not," she said. "But sometimes he sure acts like it."

"Well, we can all act immaturely when we are disappointed. Do you ever do that?"

Annie thought a moment. "Yeah. I guess so."

"And Justin. Did you have your name on that piece of bacon?"

"No, but I wanted it."

"Well, Annie got to it before you did. Would you like me to fix you another piece?"

"Nah. Not really. But can I have the last piece tomorrow?"

"Annie?"

"Sure. I guess so."

Later Laura helped Blackie and Tom with the dishes. The kids were in the TV room.

"Why didn't you just hit her?" Laura said as she stacked plates in the dishwasher. "That would have shut her up. A good backhand would have taught her not to pick on Justin."

Blackie smiled a little. "Maybe. But it would have also taught her some other things. Anger. Fear. That disagreements are settled with violence. I don't want her to learn that. I want her to see that you can talk things out. Be considerate. Caring."

Another time, Laura was having dinner with Blackie's family. Blackie always fixed food Laura had hardly heard of. This night she had made curried lamb. With Laura's help, she had worked on it all afternoon.

Six o'clock was dinner time. When they sat down, Annie was not there.

"Late again," Tom said.

Blackie began passing the food. "Let's get started," she said.

Annie burst in a few minutes later.

"Sorry, sorry," she said quickly. She was out of breath from running. "Jenny got a new puppy. I forgot the time."

Tom passed her the meat. "I can understand that. But we've talked about being late for dinner before. Right?"

Annie frowned. "Yeah. Right."

"So. What are the consequences?"

Annie frowned deeper. "I do the dishes tonight." She looked brighter. "I'll work on it. OK?"

Just then Justin reached for a roll. His arm hit his glass of milk. It toppled over with a crash. Milk spread across the dark wood of the table like a white river. Laura braced for the reaction.

"Geez," Tom groaned. Then he smiled. He got up and grabbed a dish cloth. He handed it to Justin. "OK, partner. Let's clean it up."

Justin smiled up at his dad. "We'll get this cleaned up in no time, eh Dad?"

"Sure will, partner. Want some more milk?"

The next month the Blackmores took Laura to Stanley Park. "Gee, it's really fun when you come," Justin said that morning. "We get to go to all kinds of neat places."

Laura had never seen the ocean, much less a whale. The fish and sea mammals in the aquarium fascinated her. She fell back in disbelief, squealing, when the killer whale leapt out of the water.

Afterwards, they walked through the zoo. Justin was running ahead of them. Suddenly he disappeared. Mr. Blackmore looked a little worried. He hurried on ahead. The rest followed.

In front of them, Justin had climbed a low wall and sat on top. Below him giant white polar bears paced back and forth. They looked at him curiously. Blackie gasped a little.

Tom rushed up to the wall. "Get down, please." His voice wasn't harsh. But there was an edge to it. Justin looked around at his father.

"But they're bears, Dad. Just like my teddies."

Mr. Blackmore moved slowly up to where Justin was sitting. Carefully, he put his hand out. He grabbed Justin by the collar. Now he'll get it, Laura thought.

"Climb down, Justin," Tom said again.

With Mr. Blackmore's hand on his collar, Justin slid to the ground. Tom let go. Blackie rushed up to him. Mr. Blackmore took a deep breath.

"Justin." Blackie had crouched down. Her eyes were level with Justin's. "I felt really scared when I saw you up there. I was afraid you might fall in."

Justin looked at his mother. Then he looked at the asphalt at his feet.

"Sorry, Mom. I didn't mean to scare you."

Blackie pointed up to the wall. "Do you see why I was scared?"

Justin looked over his shoulder. He looked sheepish. "Yeah."

"I wouldn't want to be the first mother on our block to have her son eaten by a polar bear."

Justin smiled a little. "Yeah," he said again.

Laura watched all this from a distance. A memory came flooding back. She had climbed up on the barn roof. Maybe she'd been six or seven. Her father had seen her. He'd screamed at her from the ground. She was scared to come down. So she climbed higher.

Her father had jumped off his tractor. He ran into the barn and climbed up the ladder. Then he crawled out the window onto the roof. He grabbed her by the foot and dragged her across the rough shingles. Her knees were scraped and bleeding. Her father grabbed her by the back of her sweatshirt and crawled back in the window. He pulled her behind him. He stood by the open window, holding her off the wooden floor by her collar.

"Wanna play on roofs, eh? Fall off and break your legs? Cost us hospital bills? I'll show you what it feels like to fall off a roof."

He jerked his arm out the window. Laura dangled 20 feet above the ground. Her shirt was tight against her throat. It pulled sharply under her arms. Her feet dangled in air. She was dazed with terror. Would he drop her?

Finally he had yanked her back into the barn. He tossed her hard on the floor.

"Next time you try that," he snarled, "I'll let you go."

That had been a long time ago. Today she was with the Blackmores. Today she was safe.

6

"It's not a big operation," Blackie said reassuringly. "I'll be out for your 15th birthday."

Laura sat in a chair in Blackie's office. She looked out the window over Blackie's shoulder. It was raining. Again.

"So why do you have to go in for the surgery?"

"Oh, it's my legs. I've always had trouble with them. Poor circulation. Varicose veins, they call them."

"Will you feel better after the operation?"

Blackie smiled. "I'd better!"

Laura frowned.

"Now don't worry," Blackie said as she sat back in her chair. "Say, have you heard the cats yowling? Just outside the gate?"

"Have I? Every night!"

"Well, Jerome says it's a mother with a litter of kittens." Jerome was the day guard on the gate. "They're wild he says."

Laura just nodded absently.

"Would you be interested in having one? As a pet?"

Laura's forehead furrowed. "But we can't have pets. That's against the rules."

Blackie smiled. "Sometimes rules can be bent. I've already checked it out with the director. I told her how much you love animals. She said it's OK."

Laura's grin was wide. "Really?" she said excitedly.

Blackie smiled back. "Really. You go on out to the gate. Jerome will let you out. See if you can catch one. It might not be that easy," she warned. "They're pretty wild."

"Jerome will let me out?" Laura looked puzzled. "No one just walks out of here."

Blackie opened her file cabinet and pulled out a file. "It's all been arranged. Shoo! I have work to do. And you have an appointment with your social worker in an hour." She opened the file and began reading.

"What about food? And litter?"

Blackie put the file down and picked up a paper bag. She handed it to Laura. Inside there were tins of cat food. There was also a small bag of cat litter.

"You can find a little box later. Now go on before you're late for your appointment."

Laura walked out of the office. She pushed the bar on the cottage door and burst outside. She ran down the walk toward the front gate. She dashed up to the guard house. Jerome was filling out forms.

"Jerome," Laura said breathlessly. "Can I really go catch one of those kittens?"

Jerome was a big man with a huge pot belly. His blue tie hung far out over his white shirt. Laura had gotten to know him when she left for weekends with Blackie. He always waved and smiled. Now he turned to her with a wink.

"Little lady, I don't know who you know," he said. "But I've worked here 21 years. No girl has ever been given permission to leave here on her own. Much less to get a kitten." He turned to her with a smile. "You must be something pretty special."

Jerome hoisted himself up from his stool. He pushed opened the door and pulled out his keys. He walked to the gate and slid the key into a padlock. It opened and he pulled the gates apart.

"They're right down in that ditch." Jerome pointed to his left. "Maybe a hundred yards."

Laura stepped hesitantly through the gate. She looked back at Jerome. He smiled at her. She walked on the sidewalk along the ditch. She studied the weeds. But she thought about running. She could do it. She could just keep on going. Maybe they wouldn't catch her.

But what about Blackie? And anyway, where would she run to?

Just then she heard a mewing. It came from a dry drain pipe just ahead. Laura slid down into the ditch. She crept up quietly. She saw the mother cat. It jumped up when it saw her. Four tiny kittens stood on their little legs. They peered up at her. The mother yowled. Two skittered away into the high grass. Another tumbled over to its mother. But one didn't move. It stared straight at her. It arched its back and spit at her. Laura laughed out loud. It was orange and looked like a miniature tiger. She moved gently toward it. She held out a hand. The kitten took a teeny swipe at it. Laura quickly slipped the hand underneath the kitten.

The kitten squirmed and squealed. But Laura held on gently. She held the trembling cat to her chest. It was warm. She petted it. It seemed to calm down. Then to Laura's surprise it began to purr.

Laura carried the kitten in her arms. She walked slowly back to the gate. Jerome was waiting for her.

"Look, Jerome," Laura said. "What do you think?"

Jerome studied the tiny cat peeking above Laura's arms.

Jerome looked serious. He shook his head. "I don't know, Laura. He looks pretty fierce."

Laura laughed and walked back through the gates. She barely heard them clang shut behind her.

She took the little kitten to her room. She put it on her bed. It looked up at her uncertainly. She took a bowl from the bag and opened a can of cat food. The kitten sniffed the air with its little nose. It walked over to the edge of the bed. It looked down at the floor in dismay.

"Mew," it said, still staring at the floor.

Laura laughed and picked it up. She put it on the floor. It raced over to the bowl. It ate hungrily.

"Well, little cat. What'll we call you?" She studied him attacking his food. His little orange tail swished furiously. "How about Tiger? Not very original. But it'll do."

Laura looked at the clock on her dresser. It was nearly 2:00 p.m. "OK, Tiger. Here's the litter box." Laura pointed to a shoe box she'd filled with litter. "I have to go see Mrs. Cooper. I'll be back soon."

Tiger was still tearing at his food as she left. Laura walked down the hall to Mrs. Cooper's office. It was right next to Blackie's. She met with Mrs. Cooper once a month or so. But this was different. Mrs. Cooper had asked her for a special meeting.

Laura knocked on the door. "Come in," Mrs. Cooper called. Laura opened the heavy wood door. She sat down in a chair facing Mrs. Cooper's desk. Mrs. Cooper was studying a file. Laura saw her name on the tab. Laura liked Mrs. Cooper. She was middle-aged. Maybe 45, Laura guessed. But she wore her yellow hair at shoulder length. And she seemed to really care how things were going. She listened. And she had a great laugh. Sometimes it would burst out like an explosion. Great guffaws that you wouldn't expect from a social worker in a grey suit.

Mrs. Cooper looked up from her file. She smiled.

"Laura. Sit down."

"I am sitting down, Mrs. Cooper."

Mrs. Cooper gave one of her great volleys of exploding laughter. "So you are," she said, still chuckling. "So you are."

Mrs. Cooper put the file down. She leaned toward Laura. "Laura, how old are you?"

"I'm turning 15 next weekend."

"Right. And that's the problem." Mrs. Cooper leaned back in her chair. "You see, we all know you don't belong here. We want to get you outside. You've got too much potential to stay cooped up in here."

Mrs. Cooper sighed. "Do you ever get any letters?"

Laura looked down at her hands in her lap. "My sisters write sometimes."

"Anyone else?" Rachel had stopped writing a year ago. Laura shook her head.

"Well, here's the problem," Mrs. Cooper said gently. "You're not 16. So we can't just release you. You are still a ward of the court. Now," Mrs. Cooper paused, "we could release you to your parents. If they would take you."

Laura looked up sharply. "I won't go back there," she said fiercely. "I'd rather stay here any day."

Mrs. Cooper sighed again. "I was afraid you'd say that." She folded her hands on top of her desk. "Was it really that bad?"

"I'll tell you how bad it was. There was an old fir tree outside of our house. My father decided to cut it down. Wanted it for fire wood. It was maybe 70, 80 feet high. Years before, he'd put an antenna on the top. For the TV. So he told me to go up and get it before he cut down the tree. I was maybe eight, nine.

"Well, you don't argue with my father. So I scrambled up. Higher and higher. Bark was getting in my eyes. I was scared to look down. But he just kept yelling at me to hurry up. So finally I got to the top. I was terrified. I was so high. And the tree kept swaying. Then I heard my father start up the chain saw down below. I felt the teeth bite into the trunk. I screamed. I grabbed the antenna. I slid down the tree. I scraped skin off my hands. Off my arms, face. Everywhere. I fell the last 10 feet to the ground.

"My father looked at me there. I was bleeding and shaking from fear. 'Baby,' he sneered. 'I was just cutting the notch.' "

Laura leaned toward Mrs. Cooper. "You see. Maybe he was just cutting the notch. Maybe he wasn't. I didn't know then. I don't know now."

Mrs. Cooper closed her eyes briefly. "OK. Home is out. You're really too old to put into a foster home. Though we could consider that. And then there is one other possibility. You lived outside of Clinton, right?"

Laura nodded.

"Did you know Clara Lawrence?"

"Is that the Mrs. Lawrence who ran the Corral Restaurant?"

"That's the one. Well, she has hired some of our graduates in the past. To work in her restaurant. She has a suite in the basement. You'd kind of be on probation. But you would be more or less on your own."

Laura stared out the window. It had started to rain again.

"And you'd be near your sisters," Mrs. Cooper concluded.

"So it's stay here until I'm 16. Get farmed out to some foster home. Or go to work for Mrs. Lawrence."

Mrs. Cooper gave a short, loud laugh. "You don't make your alternatives sound very attractive. But, yes, I guess that's about the size of it."

Laura nodded. "OK. Can I think about it?"

"Sure. Take your time."

The week passed quickly. Laura missed Blackie. But Tiger kept her occupied. She fed him. She petted him. She watched him bat balls of paper across the floor. Watched him scramble up the blanket to her bed. And at night he curled up under her arm. He purred Laura to sleep.

On Friday Laura woke up and felt the tension. It seemed to hum in the air. When she went to breakfast she saw attendants look at her and turn away. There were whispered conversations in the hall that stopped when she walked by. By night the tension had turned to something else for Laura. It was a sense of dread.

She was wide awake in her bed the next morning when the knock came. She looked at her clock. It was 7:30. She slid out from under the covers. The cold linoleum burned the soles of her feet. She walked to the door.

Mrs. Cooper was standing in the hall. This morning she was not laughing. Her hair looked unbrushed. Her mascara seemed smudged.

"Laura," she said gently. "Could you get dressed and come to my office for a minute?"

Laura turned away and dressed. She went through the motions automatically. She didn't want to think.

She walked down the hall. Mrs. Cooper's door was open. She walked in. Mrs. Cooper was standing by the file cabinet. She didn't look at Laura.

"Laura, would you shut the door please?"

Laura closed the door and sat down. She stared out the window. It was grey. Dark clouds hung low in the sky. A cold November rain ran down the window panes.

"I'm afraid I have some bad news," Mrs. Cooper began haltingly. She took a deep breath. "It's about Blackie."

Laura felt the coldness inside her spread. She said nothing.

"You knew about the operation. Well," Mrs. Cooper stopped. "Well, there were complications. With the anesthetic. That's what they use to put you to sleep. She had a reaction. She... She went into a coma. She died last night."

Laura felt her throat close. But everything else was numb.

"Blackie left you something." Mrs. Cooper walked to her desk. She picked up a large brown envelope. She handed it to Laura.

Laura opened the envelope slowly. Inside there was a white jewelry case. She opened the lid. A small gold locket shaped like a heart lay on a blue velvet bed. A gold chain was tucked underneath the velvet. There was a tiny latch on one side. Laura pulled the catch with her finger nail. The locket opened. Inside there was a picture. Laura recognized it. It had been taken at the beach. The first time she had seen the ocean. Blackie had hugged her. Blackie's husband had taken the picture.

The picture had been reduced. But Laura could make out the two faces clearly. Blackie's and Laura's heads were tilted together. They were both laughing.

Laura snapped the top closed. She held the box in her lap. She continued staring out the window.

"Mrs. Cooper," Laura said at last.

"Yes?"

"I've made a decision. I'd like to leave. I will go and work for Mrs. Lawrence."

Mrs. Cooper put her hand to her eyes. "Yes," she said, her voice cracking. "Of course. I'll make the arrangements."

"May I leave now?"

"Of course."

Laura got up and walked through the door. As she walked into the hall she remembered something. It was her 15th birthday.

7

The bus ride to Clinton seemed to drag on forever. Laura stared blankly out the window. She felt lonely. More lonely than she could ever remember. She wished Tiger was in her lap. Instead he was in the cargo section underneath her. He was in a cage Mrs. Cooper had brought.

That morning Mrs. Cooper had walked her out to the van waiting in the parking lot. She had helped Laura carry Tiger's cage. Tiger mewed and paced around inside. Laura carried her old gym bag. It was the same one she had brought with her nearly three years before.

The driver opened the side door. He tossed in the bag. He took Tiger's cage and slid it inside. He waited impatiently for Laura.

"Goodbye, Mrs. Cooper," Laura said.

Mrs. Cooper took Laura's right hand. "Goodbye, Laura. Good luck. And Laura…"

"Yes, Mrs. Cooper?"

Mrs. Cooper looked straight into Laura's eyes. "Laura, when you leave here, never look back. Do you understand?"

Laura nodded. Actually, she wasn't sure what Mrs. Cooper meant. Did she mean it literally? Shouldn't she look back as they drove out the gate?

"This is the end of this phase of your life," Mrs. Cooper continued. "Move on. Don't look back. And don't ever, ever come back. OK?"

Then Laura knew what she meant. But just to be on the safe side she kept her eyes straight ahead as they left.

Now Laura fingered the gold locket Blackie had left her. It hung around her neck on the thin gold chain. OK. She wouldn't look back. But what lay ahead? A job with a woman she didn't know. She'd be near her sisters. That would be good. What were they now? Six and eight? Annie had sent her letters. Katie had started printing little notes at the bottom. Sometimes Laura could read them. Sometimes they were just squiggles. But could she stand to see her father again?

It was night by the time the bus pulled into Clinton. A yellow half moon hid behind high broken clouds. The bus stopped by a gas station on the edge of town. The bus door opened with a loud sigh. The driver got off. Laura followed and stood quietly behind him. He took a tool and opened the cargo door. He dragged out Laura's bag. Then he pulled out Tiger's cage. Tiger stood unsteadily. He looked up at Laura. "Mew?" he asked.

Laura smiled. She took the cage and set it carefully on the pavement. "Thanks," she said to the driver.

The bus driver looked at the dark windows of the gas station.

He glanced at the deserted streets. "You got anybody meeting you?"

"Oh sure. I'll be fine."

The driver looked at her uncertainly. "You sure?"

"Sure."

He walked back to the open door. He climbed on board. The door closed with a whoosh. The driver honked twice. The bus pulled out of the gas station. It accelerated up the highway.

Now Laura looked around. There wasn't a car on the road. She walked over to a street light. At least anybody looking for her could see her. She waited for 15 minutes. Tiger curled up and went to sleep.

Well, Laura thought. Not much of a welcoming committee. Might as well walk up to the Corral.

Laura picked up her bag in her left hand. Tiger's cage was heavier. She held it in her right. She made her way into town. An occasional pickup passed. Laura looked up hopefully. Nobody seemed to notice her.

Soon she was in the town. She looked around as she walked up the sidewalk. Nothing much had changed. Still pretty much one street. Some of the stores had put up fronts on their buildings. They were supposed to look like something out of the wild west. Laura thought they just looked dumb.

Finally she saw the lights of the Corral. A few cars and trucks were parked in front. A cowboy was painted on the big glass window. He was sitting on a bronco. The bronco was bucking so hard all four feet were in the air. Steam came out of his nostrils.

The cowboy was out of the saddle. But somehow he was still twirling a rope. The rope spelled out the name of the restaurant: The Corral.

Laura walked across the street. She pushed the door open and walked in. A fish tank with a few lonely looking guppies bubbled in front of her. A row of tables ran from the window to the back wall. Behind the fish tank there was a long counter. An old cash register was at the far end. A young woman in a green uniform stood next to it. She was ringing up a bill. Laura walked up to her.

"Uh, excuse me," she began.

The girl looked up. She glanced down at the cage. Then she looked back at Laura. "Can I help you?"

Laura put her bag down. "I hope so. I'm looking for Clara Lawrence."

The girl pushed a swinging door open behind her. She stuck her head through.

"Clara!" she yelled. "Somebody here to see you!" She stepped back to the register. She smiled briefly at Laura. Then she went back to totalling her bills.

Soon the door burst open. A woman the size and shape of a giant potato waddled out. She wore a soiled apron that had once been white. It stretched across her wide middle. A white cap was pushed back on her grey hair. She walked up to the counter and grinned at Laura.

"What can I do for you, young lady?" Her voice was hoarse and raspy. But not unfriendly.

"I'm Laura Martin."

The woman wiped her right hand on her apron. She poked it across the counter.

"And I'm Clara Lawrence."

Laura took the woman's hand reluctantly. "Yes. I know. I am supposed to work for you."

Suddenly the woman's eyes grew wide. She smacked herself on her forehead. "Laura Martin. From Willingdon. Of course. But what are you doing here, honey? You're not due in until tomorrow night."

"No, ma'am. I got in tonight."

Clara smacked herself on the forehead again. "Well aren't I as useless as tits on a bull. I thought for sure it was tomorrow. Well, here you are. So I guess you're right. Well, anyway, let's get you settled. Oh, by the way," Clara interrupted herself for a moment. She nodded at the girl still working at the till. "Patty, this is Laura. Laura, Patty."

Patty looked up and smiled. "Howdy. Welcome to the Corral. Home of the best barbecued beef sandwich in Clinton."

"That's 'Best barbecued beef sandwich in the West,' sweetie," Clara corrected.

Patty's eyes twinkled. "Oh, right."

"OK, OK. Enough chit chat. Patty, get that bill figured out. At this rate the customers will still be here for breakfast by the time you get them their change." Clara looked back at Laura. "As for you, let's get you settled. Come on down into the basement."

Laura picked up her bag and Tiger's cage. "Is it dark?"

"What? The basement? Nah. Not once you turn on the lights."

Laura followed Clara through the swinging door. Clara led her to a stairway. She turned on a light and motioned Laura down the stairs. Laura squeezed by her. She walked carefully down the wooden steps. At the bottom there was a large room. A door was ajar at the far end. It opened into the bathroom. A double bed was against the wall on her right. A bright red and white checked quilt covered it. There were two small windows near the ceiling.

Laura put the cage down. The floor was covered with hideously ugly bright orange shag carpeting. Clara saw Laura staring at it.

"It was on sale." Clara shrugged her rounded shoulders. "Besides, I thought it would brighten the place up."

Clara stood halfway down the stairs. "Now listen, honey. I can see you're attached to that cat. And I don't have anything against them. But if it pees on the carpet it becomes the special of the day. Got it?"

Laura looked up, alarmed. Clara laughed out loud.

"Hey, lighten up. I know you've had a rough time. But you got to untie your knickers a little."

Laura frowned. She didn't know what Clara was talking about. None of her underwear was tied up in a knot.

"OK, listen, kid. Just relax. Why don't you unpack? Then come upstairs. We'll get you something to eat. Have a little talk. How about it?"

Laura put her few clothes in a small dresser next to her bed. Then she let Tiger out of his cage. Tiger sniffed around the edges of the room. Laura took the little litter box out of the cage. She put it in a corner.

"This'll have to do for now, Tiger." Tiger looked up at her. "I'll get you something better tomorrow. But use it, OK?" Laura added worriedly. "I don't want you to wind up in some soup."

Tiger seemed satisfied. He walked over to the bed. He scrambled up the quilt and curled up on the pillow. By the time Laura was unpacked, Tiger was asleep.

Laura walked back upstairs. She studied the kitchen. A large stove spread across one wall. Baskets for french fries sat in cooling fat. A big, two-doored stainless steel refrigerator was on the other side. A square island was in the middle of the kitchen. It was covered in wood. A large sink occupied the far end. A sprayer dangled from a hose that looped up and over the sink. Actually, Laura thought, the whole place looks pretty clean.

Clara bustled through the swinging doors. "Oh, there you are. Just pushing out the last few customers. Come on out. Sit down and have a cup of coffee." She looked at Laura uncertainly. "You do drink coffee, don't you?"

"Well, sometimes."

Clara looked relieved. "Good, good. Pour yourself a cup. It's probably thick enough to stand a spoon in. But it'll warm you up."

Laura wasn't at all sure she wanted to drink coffee that would hold up a spoon. But she walked outside and sat in a chair covered in shiny red plastic. Patty must have gone. The restaurant was deserted.

It wasn't long before Clara pushed through the door. She poured herself a cup of coffee at the counter. Then she poured a second cup. "Cream and sugar?" she called.

Laura nodded. Clara brought the two cups over to the table. Laura's coffee was light tan. Clara pulled another chair up and settled into it.

"Now then. Let's catch up a little," she began. "You're George Martin's oldest girl. They sent you to Willingdon. You stayed in touch with them?"

Laura shook her head. "Just my sisters."

Clara took a sip of her coffee. "He's one of the meanest son-of-a-bitches I've ever met. I don't blame you for winding up in Willingdon. Suspect it had less to do with you and more to do with that lousy old man of yours."

Laura said nothing.

"Anyway, I want to let you know that Social Services has been out there. I got this second hand. Apparently they threatened to pull the girls if he didn't straighten up. Understand things are better now."

Laura glanced up. "Good," she whispered.

"Now what else do you want to know?"

"How about Rachel Thomas? I stayed with her for a while. She wrote me. Then the letters just stopped. A little over a year ago."

Clara held her cup in her two hands on the table. She stared at it for long time.

"Funny story. She died."

"Oh!" It came out low, like a murmur of pain.

"Yeah. Pretty strange. No one really knows what happened. They found her in her corral. She had apparently been breaking a horse. Her neck was broken."

"Rachel was the best rider in the valley," Laura protested. "No horse could buck her. Besides, she'd brought those horses up since they were colts."

"Yeah. I know. And there was some other stuff, too."

"Like what?"

"Oh, cuts, bruises. The coroner said they could have been caused by the fall. But they might not have been too."

"It could have been murder?"

Clara looked up. "Officially accidental death. No one knows for sure."

Laura was quiet for a long time. "And Sarah. What happened to her?"

Clara shrugged. "Went to live with her dad. Somewhere in the Yukon. Don't know where. Maybe some of the kids do."

There was a long silence. Laura and Clara sipped their coffee. Finally Clara looked up. "You know, it's not going to be easy."

"What's that?"

"Coming back here. It's not going to be easy. The kids…" Clara hesitated. "The kids will say things. Call you 'jailbird,' stuff like that. I know. I've seen it before."

Laura stirred her coffee silently. She didn't say anything. She didn't know what to say.

"Are you going out there?"

"Where?"

"Your parents' place."

Laura took the spoon out of the cup. She set it carefully on the table. A little pool of coffee collected on the grey Formica.

"Yeah." Laura took a deep breath. "I'd really like to see my sisters."

"You afraid?"

Laura looked up. "Yeah."

Clara reached over the table. She took Laura's hand in her pudgy fingers. "I'll take you out. Some afternoon. Patty can look after the place. But take your time. No rush." She let go of Laura's hand. "Now get to bed. You have to wait tables for breakfast. We open at 6:00 sharp."

Laura got up and walked through the door to the kitchen. Clara followed her. She walked to the refrigerator.

"Laura," Clara called, pouring some milk in a bowl. "That little cat of yours is probably hungry."

Laura came back and took the bowl. "Thanks," she said. Then she looked up into Clara's eyes. "Thanks for everything."

8

Dishes clattered as Patty emptied her tray. Laura was up to her elbows in soapy water. She had been at the Corral for two weeks. During that time she had waited tables, washed dishes and begun cooking. Clara said she had real cooking talent. Right now, Laura wished she was flipping burgers or roasting a beef in the oven. She'd been washing dishes for an hour. She could barely keep up.

"God," Patty said. "Saturday lunch. The place is packed. They just keep coming."

Clara was working the grill. "That clatter of dishes is the sound of money, little ladies. Don't forget it."

"Well then," Patty called back. "Maybe you'll up our wages."

"Ha! Fat chance. You should be grateful I keep you on. Only out of the goodness of my heart, you know."

"Well, we are eternally grateful for your kindness," Patty said. "Minimum wage plus half our tips. You are truly a generous boss. Generous, generous, generous."

"Well," Clara sounded hurt. "Don't forget the free meals."

"The food is so bad here you should pay us to eat it," Patty joked.

Clara laughed. She jerked her head toward the door. "Well, just don't tell them that."

Patty had cleared the last of the plates and glasses from her tray. She leaned against the counter next to the sink.

"So what do you think of Larry?" she said to Laura.

Laura looked up. Sweat dripped down her forehead. A drop was suspended from the end of her nose.

"Larry? You mean that guy who hangs around with Paul?" Paul was Patty's boyfriend. He and Larry usually closed up the place waiting for Patty to finish her night shift. Clara gave them free coffee.

"Yeah. He kind of likes you."

Laura's head whipped around. The sweat flew from her nose. Her face was bright red. Patty was pretty sure it wasn't just from the hot dishwater.

"He does? How do you know?"

Patty looked smug. "He told me. Last night."

Laura turned back to the sink. Her heart was beating faster. "Actually, he seems kind of like a dork."

Patty gave a little shrug. "Yeah, he's a little dorky. Maybe it's the glasses. He really should get better glasses. But he's got a car. And he likes you."

That was a plus, Laura thought.

"There is one thing," Patty added. "He's real religious."

Laura thought about her father. "That's OK."

"He's pretty nice. A little odd, but nice."

Laura scrubbed harder at the dishes.

That afternoon the crowd thinned. There were just a few old men sitting in booths. They were smoking and nursing coffees. Laura was sitting on a stool. She was finishing a bacon, lettuce and tomato sandwich. Clara bustled through the door.

"Oh, hi. Things are pretty slow out there." Clara paused. "I had a little time. Thought you might want me to run you out to your folks' farm this afternoon."

Laura's heart jolted.

"This afternoon?"

"Yeah. Like now."

Laura had stopped chewing. "Do they even know I'm here?"

"Yeah. I saw your mom a week or so ago. I spoke with her. She'd gotten a letter from Willingdon. You know, she looked sad. She said she was sorry for the way things worked out."

"My mother? My mother said that?"

"Yeah, more or less. I think she'd like to see you. She said your sisters missed you."

Laura sat quietly on the stool for a long moment. "OK," she said at last. "Let me change and we'll go out."

It had been three years since Laura had travelled the road to the farm. But she remembered every turn, every tree. As they got closer she felt the fear grow inside her. When Clara turned her old Ford pickup into the drive, Laura's heart was beating fast. It was Saturday. Maybe her father wasn't there. Maybe he was away trading horses. Maybe it would just be her mother and sisters.

They pulled up in front of the old farm house. It hadn't been painted since Laura had last been there. There seemed to be a few more old cars in the back. Weeds grew high around their rusted bodies. Firewood was stacked on the front porch.

Laura followed Clara to the front door. It had never been painted. It was darkened by the weather and stained by dirty hands. She heard a noise inside when Clara knocked. She prayed it wasn't her father.

A little girl opened the door. She had short brown hair. She looked like Laura in her grade one school picture. "Yes?" she said.

"Hi, Katie. I'm Mrs. Lawrence. Do you know who this is?"

The little girl looked at Laura for the first time. She shook her head.

"This is Laura. This is your sister."

The girl's eyes widened. Her face split in a huge smile. "Laura!" she cried. She pushed the door open and ran to Laura. Laura kneeled down. Katie jumped into her arms.

Laura felt her throat close. She swallowed hard. "Hi there, Katie," she said softly.

Laura heard a noise at the door. She looked up. It was her mother. Her mother was wearing an old red apron. She was twisting a tissue in her right hand.

"Hello, Laura."

"Mom."

Laura's mother hesitated. Then she pushed the door open. "Come on in. Both of you."

Clara and Laura walked inside. The same old brown sofa sat in the middle of the living room. A crocheted throw in pink and light green was spread over it to cover the holes. The walls needed paint.

There was an awkward silence. "Let me get you some tea," Laura's mother said at last.

"That's OK. Really," Laura said. "Where's Annie?"

"She's doing chores."

Katie still held Laura's hand tightly. "Oh, Laura. Let me show you the new kittens. They're in the barn." Katie began tugging Laura toward the front door.

"OK," Laura laughed. "Let's see them."

Laura took a deep breath as they walked across the dirt drive to the barn.

"What happened to Mrs. Kitty?" Laura asked. Mrs. Kitty was Laura's old cat.

"Oh," Katie said, looking at the ground. "Dad killed her. He said she didn't catch mice anymore." Katie brightened. "But the new kittens are real cute."

Just then Laura heard a voice. It was coming from inside the barn. "I told you to have that stall cleaned out," the voice growled. "You have it done in an hour or I'll give you a taste of the strap. You understand, girl?"

Her father turned out of the darkness of the barn. He stopped still. He stared at Laura. Laura felt faint. She closed her eyes, got her balance. Katie tugged on her hand.

"Come on, Laura!"

Her father walked toward her.

"You go ahead, Katie," Laura said. "I want to speak to Dad. I'll be right there."

Katie went reluctantly into the barn. She didn't look at her father as she passed him.

"So, you're back," Laura's father muttered.

His face was still covered in a curly beard. He looked like he was wearing the same old green vest she'd seen him in at Rachel's. His tiny eyes looked wary.

Laura stared at him. Her heart rate was back to normal. She felt surprisingly calm, clear. Things had changed, and they both knew it.

"Not back here. I'm working for Clara Lawrence in town. I came to see the girls."

Laura's father grunted.

"I'm going to be spending as much time with them as I can," she said evenly. "They're not going to go through what I did. I don't want to hear about any straps. And don't ever talk to Annie like that again."

Laura saw her father's eyes blaze. Then there was something else there Laura hadn't seen before. Confusion. Uncertainty.

"And if they mention any abuse, of any kind, I'm going straight to Social Services." She glared at her father. "I mean it."

"Laura!" A tall, thin girl burst out of the barn.

Laura held her father's eyes for a moment longer. Then she turned to Annie running toward her.

"Annie!" she shouted, opening her arms. Annie rushed to her and hugged her hard.

"I'm so glad you're back!"

Laura glanced at her father. He was staring at the house.

"So am I, Annie. So am I."

9

"So, you and Larry going out again tonight?"

Patty was picking up an order from Laura. Laura had been cooking more and more. Clara said Laura was a better cook than she was. But Laura thought Clara also wanted to take it a little easier. Now she spent most of her time running the till. And chatting with all the customers.

"Yeah, we'll probably go out somewhere."

Patty had a little grin on her face. "Must be getting serious. You've been out with him almost every night for the last two months."

Laura kept her eyes on the hash browns she was cooking on the grill.

"Well?" Patty persisted.

"Well what?"

"Well, is it getting serious?"

"Well, it's really none of your business, now is it?"

Patty arched her eyebrows. "Oh, touchy, eh? Must be more serious than I thought."

Now Laura turned to Patty. She tried to sound angry. But a smile played around her lips.

"Do you want these hash browns on the plate? Or on your head?"

The past two months had been the best Laura could remember. She spent almost every weekend with her sisters. They walked and talked. Sometimes they rode deep into the rolling hills. Her mother wasn't exactly friendly. But at least she was polite. Maybe a little ashamed.

And her father stayed away from her.

Larry had asked her out for the first time seven or eight weeks earlier. She slid in next to Patty at a booth late one night. Larry was sitting with Paul. After a little small talk, there was an awkward silence. Finally Paul jabbed Larry in the side.

"Go on," he said.

Larry cleared his throat. He stared hard at the Formica table top. "Umm, Laura," he had stammered nervously. "I…" He stopped.

Paul rolled his eyes in exasperation. "What he's trying to say is that he'd like to take you out."

"Sure," Laura said.

Larry looked up. "You would? You would go out with me?"

Laura shrugged. "Sure. Why not? Not much else happening."

And that had started their romance. Of course, it wasn't much of a romance. Larry hardly touched her. Instead they spent hours in his pickup, cruising up and down Clinton's one street. They would stop and talk with other carloads of people. Sometimes they would talk a little to each other. But not much.

Laura didn't mind. At least she was with someone who seemed to care for her. And he had a truck. And he was 24, eight years older than she was. He seemed mature. Able to take care of her.

Larry had a small farm outside of town. It had been his parents. But they had retired to Kamloops. Now Larry ran a few head of cattle and raised some hay. Laura began to think about living with Larry on the ranch. Her own place. Kids. A few horses. It was almost too much to hope for.

Laura wished Larry would be a little warmer with her. Sometimes he would put his arm around her shoulders when they drove. Laura would snuggle up against him. But when she did he seemed to pull away. He'd quickly take his arm down and grip the steering wheel hard. But Laura was patient. She could wait.

The dinner rush was finally over. Clara had said Laura could leave at 9:00. She peeled off her apron and went downstairs. She took a quick shower to wash the grease out of her hair. Then she dressed. She hesitated. Then she picked out the push-up bra she'd just bought through a catalog. She pulled out a blue silk shirt. She buttoned it up. Then she unbuttoned the two top buttons. She smiled in the mirror. She wasn't large, but the bra gave her some nice cleavage.

Larry obviously thought so too. When she walked through the doors he was sitting at a booth with a cup of coffee. When he saw her his eyes widened. He could hardly keep from staring at her chest.

She smiled at him. "Ready?"

"Yeah, yeah," he stammered. "You bet."

"Want to finish your coffee?"

His eyes looked slightly glazed. "Huh?"

"Your coffee."

"Oh. Nah. It's OK."

They walked out to his truck. Laura slid into the passenger's side. She looked through the windshield. It was early spring. A full moon shone in a sky full of stars. The smells of awakening plants drifted through the open window. Larry climbed in on the other side.

"Larry, it's such a beautiful night. What do you say we ride up to the ridge?" The ridge was a high bluff, 20 minutes from town. It looked over the river and rolling hill country for miles.

Larry seemed to gulp. "OK. Sure. I guess so."

As they drove, Laura slipped closer to Larry. At first he pressed himself against the door. Then he seemed to change. He put his arm around her shoulder. He pulled her to him. She could hear his shallow, quick breathing.

They were the only truck at the bluff. Larry pulled to the end of the gravel road. He yanked on the parking brake and turned off the lights. He turned off the ignition.

Suddenly he was all over her. She was forced against the far door.

"Whoa," she whispered. "Take it easy, honey."

He slowed down, but Laura had to help him unbutton her

blouse. She was afraid he would rip it. He pulled away and began to tear off his clothes. Laura slipped out of her jeans.

It wasn't what she had thought making love for the first time would be like. She had imagined long embraces, gentle kisses. But he came at her with an intensity that scared her. He seemed to radiate ferocious heat.

It was all over quickly. He lay still for a moment. Then he pulled back and sat up. He lowered his head to the steering wheel. He seemed to be gasping. Crying.

Laura pushed herself up. She put her hand on his bare shoulder. He recoiled.

"I'm sorry," he sobbed. "I couldn't help it."

Laura looked puzzled. "What's to be sorry for? There were two of us you know."

"No, no. It's me. I'm weak. I'm so ashamed. The Lord will punish me."

"What are you talking about?"

" 'The eyes of the Lord are in every place, keeping watch upon the evil and the good.' Proverbs 15. He knows."

"It's OK, Larry," Laura said soothingly.

"It's *not* OK. The Lord said to avoid harlots. 'Let not your heart decline to her ways. Go not astray in her paths. For she hath cast down many. Many strong men have been slain by her. Her house is the way to hell.' "

Laura pulled away. She slipped on her bra and began buttoning up her blouse.

"I'm not sure I like being called a harlot."

Larry turned to her. His face was streaked with tears. He was clearly in great pain.

"I don't mean you. It's me. I have lusted for you for weeks. I have sinned in my heart. I tried going to prayer meetings. But it didn't help."

Laura finished getting dressed in silence. Larry took his clothes and opened the door. In the quick flash of the overhead light she caught a glimpse of his bare buttocks as he rushed out the door. She smiled.

When Larry climbed back in the truck he was changed, calmer. He started the motor. They drove quietly back toward town.

"Laura," Larry said at last. "We have to get married."

Laura was startled. "Do I have anything to say about it?"

"It's the only way to atone."

"You know, Larry. I don't really feel I have anything to atone for."

"We're all sinners. My parents showed me that. They tried to beat it out of me. But the devil is determined."

Larry had never talked much about his family. "Did they beat you often?"

"Oh yes. But only when I deserved it."

There was more silence. Laura thought of the desperate young man next to her. Her hopes for a home. To have a life. Her life. She thought about his farm. It was a way out.

They pulled up in front of the restaurant. Laura stared out the side window.

"Well?" Larry asked.

"Do you love me, Larry?"

"Sure. Of course I do. I wouldn't have made love to you if I didn't."

Laura looked at nothing through the window.

"I'll let you know."

"Soon?"

"Soon."

Laura opened the door and climbed down from the truck. The full moon had dropped behind the hills. The night sky was black.

10

They were married two weeks later. It was a small service at Larry's church. The minister seemed kind. He smiled widely. Patty was the bridesmaid. Clara sat in a pew dabbing at her eyes with a Kleenex. Just as the service began, Laura heard the church door creak open. She looked. It was her mother and two sisters. Annie waved.

Laura smiled and turned toward the minister.

Laura had visited the ranch. But living there was different. Now she saw how run down it was. The clogged drains. The fences that needed repairing. The dirty floors. The curtains that hadn't been washed in years.

But Tiger loved it. He stalked mice for hours in the old barn. He prowled in the high grass around the house and looked more like a tiger than ever. But for some reason he didn't like to be inside when Larry was there. When Larry tried to pet him, he would spit and squirm away. Larry would laugh nervously.

"I'm sure he'll get over it," Laura said. But he never did.

The farm wasn't much. But it was Laura's. And she threw herself into cleaning, painting and repairing it. Her years of forced work on her parents' ranch was at least paying off now. She could fix leaky faucets. Repair broken equipment. Pitch hay bales.

Once Larry and Laura had been out in a hay field. Larry was taking a local dairy farmer to look at hay. The truck wouldn't start.

"Oh, great," Larry muttered. "It's a long walk back."

Laura had climbed out of the cab. "Open the hood." Laura grabbed a screwdriver. She tinkered for a few minutes.

"Try it again."

Larry turned the engine over. It exploded into life. Laura got back into the truck.

"How'd you do that?" Larry asked.

"Just the solenoid," Laura said. "Nothing really."

Larry watched Laura with amusement and awe. Where she understood engines, he didn't know a piston from a crankshaft. She was a bundle of energy. He preferred reading the Bible and watching TV. She worked long into the evenings. Larry went to prayer meetings three nights a week.

One night Larry came in late. Laura was washing a long-neglected linoleum floor. She wiped sweat from her forehead.

"Larry, how about staying home and helping out. There's a ton of stuff to do."

He grinned. "You seem to be doing OK."

Laura leaned on the mop. "That's not exactly the point. It would be nice to get some help."

Larry lowered his eyes. "These meetings are very important to me. Why don't you come with me?"

"Larry, I've got too much to do to sit around and read the Bible aloud. And sing hymns and testify. I can pray on my own." She paused. "What do you get out of them, anyway?"

Larry sank down in an old easy chair. He sighed.

"The Lord tells me to do it."

Laura shook her head wearily. "It's pretty hard to argue with the Lord."

He looked up at her. His eyes were bright. "I'm a sinner."

Laura raised her hands in exasperation. "You keep telling me that. Maybe you should give yourself a break."

"You don't know." He closed his eyes. "Believe me, the only good thing about me is Jesus." He opened his eyes. They were bright and dancing. "And when I am praying, testifying, I become something else. I'm part of something bigger. Something good. I can lose myself."

Laura stood the mop in the bucket. She walked over to Larry. She stroked his hair.

"You can be kind, caring, Larry. I've never seen you do one mean thing. Don't run yourself down like this. It bothers me."

The flame died in Larry's eyes. Now it was replaced by something else. Darkness.

"You don't really know me. The dreams." He covered his eyes with his right hand. "The fantasies." He looked back up at her. "You don't know me."

"Stop it," she said gently. "I married you, didn't I?"

"Then help me," Larry pleaded. "I'm afraid. I'm a sinner. And the Lord says, 'If you walk contrary to me, I will walk contrary unto you. I will punish you seven times for your sins. I will send the pestilence among you. Ye shall be delivered into the hand of the enemy. And ye shall eat the flesh of your sons. And the flesh of your daughters shall you eat.' Leviticus 26."

"Stop it, Larry," she said again. "I will help you." She pulled his head to her breast and hugged him. "Stop it, now."

Laura hated to see Larry this way. It seemed to come and go. Most of the time she was able to forget it. There was so much to do. And there was the joy of having her own place. Sometimes she found herself smiling for no reason.

And then Laura found that she was pregnant.

For Laura, it was one more thing to be happy about. But Larry seemed agitated. Angry. "That's just what we need," he said, shaking his head. "Another mouth to feed. We can barely make it now."

He was right, of course. But Laura didn't care. She worked even harder. She cleaned out the bedroom upstairs. Painted it a soft pink. She bought a baby bed from the second hand store. Milked the cows. Kept the books for the hay sales. Sat knitting clothes in a rocking chair with Tiger on her lap.

Larry, however, seemed to do less and less. He slept late. When he was up he did a few chores. Then he read his worn Bible. Every night now he went into town for a prayer meeting.

A month before the baby was due, Larry brought up names. They were sitting at the old wood table eating dinner. Laura seemed to have less and less to say to Larry. There was a long silence.

"I guess," Larry said, chewing a mouthful of roast beef. "I guess we should talk about names."

Laura kept her eyes on her plate. She carefully speared green peas.

"I want something biblical. If it's a boy, David, Benjamin. Maybe Matthew."

Laura took a drink of milk. "It's going to be a girl."

Larry stopped chewing. "Now, you don't know that."

"It's going to be a girl," Laura repeated. She said it calmly. Matter of fact.

Larry looked annoyed. "Well, all right. Let's say it is. How about Esther, or Ruth?"

"Rachel," Laura said.

"Rachel's nice. Wife of Jacob. Mother of Joseph and Benjamin."

Laura looked up. Her voice was light. But her eyes were clear, determined. "Her name's going to be Rachel Martha."

"Well," Larry whined. "Martha's OK, too. Mary's sister. But don't I get a say?"

Laura gave him a small smile.

"No."

Rachel Martha was born in November. Laura thought she was beautiful. Laura had just turned 17.

But the baby seemed to create even more distance between Larry and Laura. He begged Laura to baptize Rachel. But Laura stood her ground. "She'll make up her own mind. When she's old enough."

Larry stayed away more and more. In some ways Laura didn't

care. She had her baby and the farm. But at times she felt lonely. Isolated. Patty came out and visited. And occasionally Clara would bring out Laura's sisters. That was the best time. She loved watching Annie and Katie play with the baby. Once Laura's mother visited. It was awkward for both of them. Laura wanted to talk to her. But she couldn't. Not yet.

At first Tiger was a little jealous. He sulked outside for three nights after the baby came home. Then on the fourth morning Laura found a dead mouse on the floor by the baby's bed. At first she had recoiled. Blood streaked its grey fur. She picked it up by its tail and glanced around. Tiger lay purring in the rocker. He looked at her proudly.

Laura laughed. "A peace offering, Tiger? How thoughtful."

After that Tiger saw himself as Rachel's guardian. Often he slept in her bed. Even when Rachel got older and pulled his fur, Tiger never scratched.

11

Laura sat back heavily in the chair. Bills and papers covered the desk in front of her. She sighed heavily.

"Larry, if we don't do something we're going to lose the farm."

Larry was sitting on the couch. He was watching a football game on TV. Rachel was sitting in her playpen. She was banging wooden pegs with a hammer.

Larry glanced around. "What do you want me to do about it?"

"You could do more around the place for starters."

"Quit harping, woman!" he said angrily.

"Larry," Laura said carefully. "I don't mean to harp. But we can't go on this way. We're not making enough to pay the bills."

"I put my trust in the Lord."

"Doesn't it say something about the Lord helping those who help themselves?"

Larry glared at her from the couch.

Laura hesitated. "I'm thinking about taking a job."

Now Larry stood up. "What in God's name are you talking about?"

"Clara called today. She's taken a job cooking. At a bush camp. She's shut the Corral down for the winter. She needs some help. It's just a couple of months." Laura hesitated. "I told her I'd do it."

"No wife of mine will work!" Larry fumed.

"Larry," Laura began gently. "We have to do something. We're up to our necks in debt. We'll have to sell the place." She paused. "Do you want that?"

Larry still stood glaring at her. "So you're going to save me. And the farm. Who are you? Superwoman?"

"No, I'm not superwoman. And I don't want to leave either. But someone's got to bring in some money."

"Are you saying I'm not doing my part?"

Laura was quiet for a moment. "I'm saying it's not enough. If you keep the place up and I work outside, maybe we can make it."

Larry looked at her in silence. "And what about the baby?"

"I'll take Rachel with me. That's part of the deal."

Larry sat back down heavily. "Well, it looks like you got me again."

Laura got up from her chair. She walked over to the couch and sat next to Larry. "I'm not trying to get you. I just want to save the farm."

Larry wouldn't look at her. "When are you leaving?"

"Next Saturday. If it's OK with you."

"Does it matter if it's OK with me?"

Laura took his hand. "I'd rather you approved."

"Well, I don't approve," Larry said sulkily. "But you're going to do what you want anyway."

She gripped his hand. "It's for all of us, Larry. All three of us."

Larry grunted. "And take that damned cat with you. All it does is spit when it sees me."

"Damn!" Rusty clomped into the warm kitchen. He stomped the snow off his boots.

Laura looked up from her potatoes. She had been cooking for three weeks at the logging camp. Rachel was toddling around the kitchen. She was chewing on a piece of potato and chasing Tiger.

"What's wrong, Rusty?" Rusty was the camp manager.

"Oh, Flanagan smashed up his hand. Our only skidder driver. Trying to set a choker! I told him to stay on his machine. For Christ's sake, I told him. Let the choker man set the choker. But oh no. He's got to do it himself."

Laura looked worried. "How bad is the hand?"

"Bad enough. We had to med-evac him to Williams Lake. Now where the hell am I going to find another skidder driver?"

"Does it pay better than cooking?"

"Yeah. I reckon," Rusty muttered.

Laura kept peeling the potatoes. The peels came off in long brown strips. "If it's got an engine, I can drive it."

"Huh?" Rusty stopped stomping around. "You? You've driven a skidder?"

Laura mentally crossed her fingers. "Sure. I've been driving tractors on the farm since I was five. There isn't a piece of equipment I can't run."

"Yeah," Rusty said uncertainly. "But this ain't no farm."

Laura put down her peeler. "Try me. What do you have to lose?"

Rusty pulled his toque off. He ran his hands through his grey hair. "Hell, even if you could do it, who'd cook? And," Rusty motioned toward the baby with his chin, "what about Rachel?"

"It's only for a while. Clara can get things ready. I can still help out at dinner and breakfast. And she can look after Rachel."

Rusty grinned. "Well, lady, you've got yourself an audition."

Laura called to Clara. She was napping in the bedroom connected to the kitchen. Clara poked her head through the door. "What is it?" she asked sleepily.

"Will you look after Rachel? I've got to go run a skidder."

"A what?"

Laura laughed as she buttoned on her parka. She grabbed a yellow hard hat from a peg beside the door. "Be right back."

Laura followed Rusty out the door. They walked to the landing where logs were piled for the trucks. The skidder sat in the middle of a clearing. Laura walked over to it. It was orange. Four large tires were at the corners. The machine was hinged in the middle. It was steered by hydraulic cylinders that pushed the front left or right. A cab with a metal cage sat in front of the middle pin. A winch with a spool of thick cable was mounted high on the rear. The cable ran between big steel rollers. A large hook was attached to the end.

"Case, eh?" Laura said.

Rusty looked surprised. "You run Cases before?"

"My dad had one." Which was true, she thought. Of course it had been a little farm tractor. But it was a Case.

Laura climbed up into the cab. She settled herself into the black vinyl seat. She grabbed the gear shift lever. "Two forward gears?"

"Yeah. One reverse."

Laura nodded. She grabbed a lever on her left. "Winch?"

"Right."

"OK." She turned on the ignition. The diesel roared into life. "What do you want me to do?"

Rusty pointed down a trail. "There's a couple of loads waiting. Bob and Andy have them choked. They're down there waiting."

Laura had never operated a skidder. But it was like tractors she'd run. The steering wheel operated the cylinders. They pushed the front end right and left. She guided the big machine slowly down the trail.

When she got to the logging site, Bob and Andy looked up. Suddenly Bob grabbed Andy by his shirt sleeve. He pointed at Laura. Laura couldn't hear them. But she knew they were laughing.

Rusty came running down the trail. This was it. Laura looked around. There were three piles of logs with chokers fitted. They were behind some pretty big fir stumps. Laura didn't have much room to maneuver. She pulled the shift lever into reverse. Then she turned sharply. She turned the skidder so it was facing up the trail. She backed down to the first pile. She carefully put her tires over the lower stumps. She swiveled the skidder to straddle the higher ones. The machine neared the first pile. She stopped. Then she hit the winch lever. Cable began to spool out the rear. She stood up. Bob and Andy were staring at her. Their mouths were wide open.

"Let's go!" she yelled. Bob ran over. He grabbed the hook. He looked up at Laura. Then he pulled the cable out. He pulled it past the first and second pile. Laura could see what he was doing. She kept the cable paying out until Bob got to the third pile. He signalled. She pulled the lever. Bob slipped the hook onto the loop in the cable around the logs. He signalled again. Laura eased the winch into gear. She felt the skidder creak as the pile eased forward. She stopped by the second pile. Bob hooked the second cable loop onto the hook. She pulled the two forward. Then Bob hooked on the third. Laura had several tons of logs behind her.

Laura had seen skidders operate. She knew what she had to do. She dragged the timber closer and closer to the skidder. The winch shuddered under the weight. Slowly the butts lifted off the ground. She put on the winch brake. Then she put the skidder in gear. The skidder roared as it pulled the heavy logs up the trail. Laura caught a good look of Rusty's face. He was grinning from ear to ear.

Laura pulled the logs into the landing. Andy rushed up. He released the chokers after Laura had dropped the load to the ground. Laura pulled the skidder forward. She turned off the ignition. She climbed down from the cab.

Rusty was waiting for her. "Gotta admit. I doubted you. But I've never seen it done slicker." He stuck out his hand. "You're hired."

Over the next month, Laura learned every day. She became

better and better at maneuvering the skidder. At working the winch. At reading the choker man's signals.

And every afternoon she rushed back to help with dinner.

The men may have doubted her at first. But they grew to trust her skill.

"You know," Andy said one night as Laura was serving dinner. "You're a damned fine skidder operator, Laura." Laura blushed. Andy held up his big hand. "No, no. I mean it. More than one choker man has been killed by careless skidder operators. You're cautious." Andy's rugged face was serious. "But you get the job done." He gave Laura a clap on the shoulder. It almost knocked her over.

12

Over the next eight years Laura worked logging sites all over the interior of B.C. She became a kind of legend. The woman skidder driver with the kid and the cat. Who could cook on the side.

Laura worked for three and four months at a time. Then she returned to help with the farm.

And it needed a lot of help. Despite Laura's income, the place continued to go down hill. Larry seemed less and less interested. And he became increasingly bitter.

Every time she returned from a job it was the same. That night he would make violent love to her. When he was done he would pull away in the darkness. Then he asked the same question. "Who'd you sleep with this time?"

"Larry," she'd always say gently. "I didn't sleep with anyone. You know that."

He would just turn away and go to sleep.

He always took the money. But he hated it. Laura could see it. See the glint of anger in his eyes. The fury when he grabbed her cheques, crumpling them in his pocket.

"A woman should not be supporting her husband," he'd say. "It's not the Lord's way. I know this. He has told me so."

Laura always tried to be patient. Not to irritate him at times like this.

"I'm not supporting you, Larry. You take care of the farm. I'm just helping out."

But the gulf grew. It scared Laura. There was less and less joy in the farm. More and more tension. Anger.

But the offers kept coming in. Laura had learned how to weld. To operate cats, trucks. She was in demand everywhere. And the money was too good to pass up. Besides, they couldn't live on what the farm brought in. Not the way Larry was running it.

And then there was Rachel. She was almost 11 now. Laura knew she couldn't keep dragging Rachel from job to job. When she was staying in a town, she hired a sitter for Rachel. Sometimes she came to camp with Laura. But her schooling was spotty. Laura knew she was behind.

Laura had been back at the farm for two months when Rusty called.

"Laura!" he shouted over the phone. "Really need you up here!"

"What you got, Rusty?"

"Some steep slopes. Winter conditions. I need a skidder driver with your touch. Don't know anyone else who's got it."

"Where are you?"

"Way the hell and gone. Two hours outside of Chetwynd."

"Pay good?"

"The best."

Laura was quiet on the phone. "How long you need me?"

"Three months. Tops. Well, what do you say?"

"Let me talk to Larry. I'll get back to you tomorrow."

"OK. Gotta know by tomorrow."

That night she stayed at the dinner table after the meal. Rachel was in the living room watching TV. Larry sat at the end of the table. He was wiping up the last of the gravy with a piece of bread.

"I got a call from Rusty. He wants me to work for him for a few months."

Larry just grunted.

"Larry, we have to talk about Rachel."

Larry didn't look up. "What about her?"

"She's in school here. She's settled. I don't want to take her away. I'd like her to stay here while I'm away. With you."

Larry's head jerked up from his plate. "What?"

"Well, you are her father."

Laura saw Larry's eyes dance with emotions. There was fear, panic. And something else.

"Look, I know I've taken care of her," Laura went on. "But it's time she was settled in one place. And we need my income. I can't be here. You can. You've got lots of time."

"I… I don't know," Larry stammered.

Laura leaned forward. "I really don't think there's any other way to do it. Honestly. Can you think of something else?"

Larry stood up. He paced back and forth. He ran his fingers through his hair. "No. No, I guess not."

Laura smiled. "Good. I'm off on Saturday. You take good care of Rachel."

Rusty's camp was deep in the foothills of the Rockies. Ice bridges crossed several creeks. The cold seemed to settle on the camp like a frozen blanket. The slopes they were logging were steep and icy.

Rusty was glad to see her. Rusty had let his last skidder operator go a week before. He had tipped the machine on a high stump. It had rolled and slid down the mountain side. The man had escaped unhurt. But the machine was badly damaged.

Some of the other men weren't so happy. The first day Laura was in camp she drove the repaired skidder to the fuel tank. It was a bitter morning. At least 40 below. Laura wore heavy green rubber gloves to fuel the machine. She had on old overalls that were stained with grease. Her hair was pulled back under her orange hard hat. She wore bright yellow earmuffs. But she could still hear two fallers standing by the crummy with their saws.

"I just don't get it," one man began. Laura looked up. He had "Brad" written across the front of his hard hat. "What the hell is she doing here anyway?"

The other faller hitched his suspenders over his shoulder.

"Beats me. Rusty says she's good."

Brad heaved his red saw into the crummy. "Maybe. But why would a woman take a job like this, anyway?"

Laura slammed the nozzle into the catch on the tank. She turned toward the two men. Her hands were on her hips. She leaned toward them.

"Because women's jobs don't pay enough for me to feed my kid!" she yelled. Both men looked at her in surprise. "And there's nothing wrong with my hearing, either."

Brad opened the crummy door. "Come on, Ace."

"And one more thing," Laura yelled. The men were climbing into the truck. "I can run a skidder better than any man in these parts!"

"I'll believe that," Brad shouted from the crummy, "when I see it!"

And over the next two months Laura made believers of all of them. She worked 10, 11 hour shifts along with the men. She never complained about the slicing cold winds. She was respectful of the choker men. She complimented the fallers.

One night after dinner Laura sat exhausted in an easy chair in the TV room. Ace and Brad were playing pool in the next room. They didn't see her.

"Gotta admit it, Ace. I was wrong."

Ace knocked the two ball into a corner pocket. "I've worked with you for 10 years. You've never been wrong about anything."

"That's true. Oh, maybe once six or seven years ago."

Ace chuckled. "So what are you wrong about this second time?"

"That woman skidder. You know, she's not bad."

Ace leaned over the table. He took aim on the eight ball. "Yep. Damn near good as a man."

Brad propped his chin on his cue. He shook his head. "I've been at this more than 15 years. She's the best I've ever seen."

Laura sat low in the old chair. A smile crept across her face.

Just then Rusty walked into the room. "Laura. Call for you. I think it's your Rachel."

Laura's heartbeat quickened. She got up and walked into the office. The desk was littered with papers. The phone was perched on top of a stack of notebooks. The receiver lay on some stained bills.

Laura picked up the receiver. "Hello."

"Mommy?"

"Rachel! Honey, how did you get my number?"

"It's taped on the wall over the phone."

Rachel's voice still sounded like a little girl's. But there was something else. She thought Rachel was crying.

"Rachel, what's wrong, honey?"

There was a short silence at the other end. "I miss you, Mommy. Can you come home?" There was a pause. The voice became more insistent. Pleading. "Please?"

"But I've only got another month, sweetie. Can't you wait?"

Now there was no mistaking it. Great sobs rushed over the line. Laura hadn't heard Rachel cry since she was a baby.

Laura made a quick decision. "OK, hon. Stop crying. I'll be there tomorrow."

The sobs gave way to gentle crying. "Promise?"

"Promise. I'll be there tomorrow night. OK, pumpkin?"

"OK, Mommy."

"And pumpkin, I love you."

Laura sat quietly for a moment. She still held the receiver in her hand. Finally she hung it up. She got up and walked over to the kitchen. Rusty was drinking a cup of coffee. Peggy the cook was washing dishes.

"Rusty, I've got to leave."

"Leave! What are you talking about?"

"Rachel called. She needs me."

"Damn!" Rusty said. Then he sighed heavily. "OK. I know you wouldn't do this if it wasn't an emergency. I'll try to get Dan. That job in Quesnel should be over."

Rusty looked at Laura closely. Her face was closed, her eyes worried. "What's wrong, anyway?"

Laura stared out the square black window behind Rusty.

"I don't know."

Laura started out at four in the morning. She figured it would take her 12 hours. She had to be home by evening.

The roads were slick. Blowing snow whirled across the highway. The hours swept by. It was almost 6:00 p.m. when she pulled up to the farm house. She could see Rachel leaning over the back of the sofa. She was peering out the window. Tiger sat next to her. When Rachel saw Laura's lights, she jumped down. She ran to the door and out into the snow.

Laura got out of the truck. She caught the little girl as she rushed into her arms.

"What in the world are you doing out here in this cold? All you've got on are pajamas. And what's this? You're out here in your bare feet?"

The girl was clinging to Laura's neck. Laura gently carried her back into the house. Larry was standing inside the door. He looked startled.

"You weren't due back for another month."

Laura looked at Rachel. She was staring hard at the floor. "Ah, we finished up a little early."

Larry managed a small smile. "Well, come on in. We're just about to have some dinner. Nothing fancy. Just some Kraft Dinner and hot dogs."

"Sounds good to me."

There was little conversation that evening. Rachel hugged Tiger and sat in front of the TV. Larry read a religious magazine. He asked a few polite questions. But he seemed distracted.

"Well, sweetie," Laura said to Rachel at last. "It's bedtime. You want me to take you up?"

Rachel turned around and nodded her head.

"We can both do it," Larry said.

Laura took Rachel by her hand. She led her up the stairs. Tiger walked close behind. Laura tucked Rachel into bed. Larry stood at the door.

"Goodnight, pumpkin," Laura said. "Sweet dreams."

Rachel began to cry.

"What's wrong, honey?"

"Nothing. I'm glad you're home, Mommy."

"So am I, honey. Now go to bed."

Laura went back downstairs. Larry followed. She sat down heavily on the couch. She was exhausted.

"How'd things go?"

Larry shrugged. "Fine."

"Really?"

"I said they were fine," Larry said angrily.

"OK, Larry. I'm too tired to get into it tonight. Mind if I go to bed?"

Larry stared at the TV. He shrugged.

Laura got into her nightgown. She crawled between the sheets. She closed her eyes. Fatigue washed over her. More than anything she wanted to sleep. But she couldn't.

Laura lay perfectly still. She tried to will herself to sleep. But nothing seemed to work. Then she sensed Larry in the bedroom doorway. She felt him stare at her in the darkness. Then he was gone.

The house was old. Every step and board had a groan and a creak. She heard him make his way up the stairs. Where was he going? The bathroom was on the main floor. There was only Rachel's bedroom upstairs. Laura's heart pounded into her throat. She slipped out from the covers. She crept silently up the stairs. Rachel's door was shut. Tiger paced outside. He growled low in his throat.

Laura stood by the door for a long moment. She heard a voice inside. It was Larry. She could only make out bits and pieces.

"Our secret… Your mother loves me and… blame you… the Lord… punishment…"

Laura opened the door. Larry was naked on the bed. He was lying next to Rachel.

As soon as the door opened, Rachel was out of bed. She wore

only the top of her pajamas. She ran sobbing to Laura. She grabbed her tightly around the waist. Laura put her arm around Rachel's shoulder. She pulled Rachel closer.

Larry's eyes were wide and frightened. He raised his arm toward her.

"It's, it's not what it looks like," he stammered.

Laura stared at him. She felt like she was going to throw up.

"I beg you," he pleaded. "Please, Laura."

In the shadows his face twisted in anguish. "I knew it was wrong," he sobbed. "But I couldn't help myself." He grabbed himself by the throat. "Satan had me in his grip," he moaned. "Please don't say anything! You have to understand!"

Laura's voice was cold, loathing. "You make me sick."

"And what about you?" Larry shrieked from the bed. "You ball crusher! It's your fault. You always had to be the man! Do everything! Be everything! What about me?" He lowered his head into his hand. His body shook with ragged sobs. "What about me?"

Laura stood staring at the man. She felt no pity. Just hatred. "I hope your God can forgive you," Laura said. "I can't."

She took Rachel by the shoulders and led her down the stairs. She was quiet now. Laura gave her some of her old clothes. "Put these on, honey. We're leaving. Tonight."

"Mommy?"

Laura was stuffing clothes in a duffel bag. Most of her gear was still in the truck. "Yes, sweetie?"

"Daddy said you'd be angry. He said you'd blame me."

Laura fell to her knees. Her throat closed. She could hardly swallow. She looked into Rachel's eyes. She took the girl gently by the shoulders.

"Listen to me. You must understand this. This was not your fault. It had nothing to do with you. Understand? I'm just sorry…" Laura took a deep, shuddering breath. "I'm just so sorry I didn't see it coming." She hugged Rachel hard. "I'm so sorry."

Laura stood up. She grabbed her bags. She took Rachel's coat down from a hook. She slipped it around Rachel's shoulders. She opened the door and started for the truck.

"Mommy," Rachel pleaded. "Wait a minute."

Rachel turned back through the door. A moment later she ran back out the door. Tiger was under her arm.

13

**Help Wanted:
Hay Ranch Manager**

Needed immediately. Resident manager of 1000 acre hay farm near Kamloops. Must have extensive hay farming experience. Must be able to operate range of farm equipment. Ability to maintain equipment an asset. Some welding required. Reply to: Raymond Rivera. Box 189, Kamloops, BC. V2N 1Y7

"Hey, Clara. Have a look at this." Laura and Clara were in the kitchen of the Corral. Laura held up the paper as Clara peered over her shoulder. "What do you think?"

Clara read the ad. "For you?"

"Of course for me. Who else? Rachel and I can't stay here forever."

Clara wiped her hands on her apron. "Why not?"

Laura looked around and smiled. "Clara, I can't tell you how grateful I am to you. You've been wonderful. I don't know what we would have done if you hadn't been here. But it's been almost a year. I have to get a place of my own. For Rachel."

Clara looked sad. "It's not like you haven't done your part. Cooking. Waitressing."

Laura turned around in her chair. She reached out and took the older woman's hand. "Clara, I'm almost 30. I've got a 12-year-old daughter. As generous as you've been, I don't want to stay in your basement for good. I don't want to just get by on what you can give me for a little cooking."

Clara pouted. "Why don't you go back skidding? Leave Rachel with me."

"I don't think so," Laura sighed. "I don't want to leave Rachel. Not yet." Laura's voice brightened. "If I could get this, we would have our own place. And we wouldn't be far away. We could drive over on weekends."

Clara walked over to the coffee pot. She poured herself a cup. "Want some?" she asked Laura.

"No thanks."

Clara walked back to the table. She sat down across from Laura. "I know it hasn't been easy for you."

Laura stared blankly at the paper in front of her. No, it hadn't been easy. She didn't show it, but inside she was still torn up. A few people had shown support. Some of them unexpected. Pastor Davidson from Larry's church visited. He told her how sorry he was. Some people, he said, came to the church for the wrong

reasons. To cover their shame. Their terrible feelings of abandon-
ment. Worthlessness. He apologized. Was there anything he
could do?

Laura appreciated his kindness. But Clara was the one she
really looked to. Laura never even had to ask. Clara cleared out the
basement for Laura and Rachel. "You just stay here as long as you
want," she said firmly.

The divorce was hard, too. She had hoped she'd never see Larry
again. He had tried to talk to her at the hearing. But she turned and
walked away. And by the time debts were taken from the value of
the farm, there wasn't much left in the settlement for Laura and
Rachel. Larry had managed to waste even the money that Laura
had brought in. And Larry hadn't made one of his child support
payments.

Rachel seemed OK on the outside. But Laura heard her crying
softly, late at night. And there was a sadness about her that scared
Laura.

Laura had thought they should press charges. She met with the
prosecutor. He shook his head. "Not enough evidence." He had
straightened his tie and picked up his files. He was anxious to get
back to Kamloops. "Besides, do you really want to put your girl
through a trial? Make her relive the whole thing? And for what?"

And then there were all the little problems she hadn't thought
of. She couldn't get a loan for a new truck without the signature of
her husband. The looks of disapproval from people in the
community.

Laura had begun to feel increasingly restless. She had to make a move. Maybe the hay farm was the answer. It was a long shot. But it was worth a try.

Clara watched her. She sipped her coffee quietly. "Do you think they'd hire a…"

"A woman?" Laura asked.

Clara pointed at her. "Exactly."

"I guess we'll find out."

"Ms. Martin. Please sit down." Raymond Rivera pointed to a chair in front of his desk. He wasn't what Laura had expected. His face was worn and lined. He wore a plaid flannel shirt and scuffed cowboy boots. His large oval belt buckle had a brass bronco bucking on it.

"Now, I want to be frank with you. When I got your application I wondered if a woman could do this job." Rivera looked over the top of his glasses. "It's very demanding work. But you gave Rusty Johnson as a reference. Rusty and I go way back. We used to rodeo together. I gave him a call." Rivera shook his head. "Bugger to track down. Anyway, after I was done talking with him, I knew I wanted to interview you."

Rivera peered over his glasses again. "But I warn you. I still have to be convinced. I own 16 ranches all over the Interior. I've hired dozens of managers." He paused for effect. "Not one has been a woman. Hell, not a single woman has ever *applied*." He sat back in his chair. "And I am a rancher. That's how I got started. So don't try to bullshit me."

Laura smiled. She had been nervous when he'd called her to

come in for the interview. But she liked this guy. She could talk to him.

"OK," she said. "Fair enough. What do you want to know?"

"Tell me about yourself."

Laura reviewed her work on her parents' farm. Her mechanical abilities. Her work in the logging camps. Her management of the farm.

"Are you tough?" Rivera asked.

Laura leaned toward him. "Mr. Rivera, do you think I could have driven a skidder for 10 years without being tough?"

Rivera laughed out loud. "Laura, I like you." Now Rivera leaned forward. "But that's not the point. Can you run a hay ranch?"

"What machinery you got?"

"Self-propelled swather…"

"Massey-Ferguson or John Deere?"

"Massey-Ferguson."

"I've run Masseys all my life. Steer with foot levers."

"And a baler of course…"

"New Holland?" Rivera nodded. "You're baling for the dairy trade. 120 pound custom bales? Wire binding?"

Rivera's eyebrows arched. "Exactly."

"I've run New Hollands and I've fixed them. You got a bale stacker?"

"Yep. John Deere."

"104 or 86 bale?" Laura asked.

"104."

"Model 17K67. Know it. I've run it."

Ray Rivera leaned over the desk. "How about irrigation. We're pulling water 700 feet from the Thompson. Twenty-one turbine stage pump."

Laura whistled. "That's a long pull. Eight inch intake?"

"Ten."

"I'll bet that sucker takes a lot of maintenance. Every time the slam valve closes, it must shake itself apart."

Rivera was smiling now. "Exactly. It splits apart at every seam. You've got to be able to weld both steel and aluminum. And the slope is almost vertical down to the river. You have to drive a D8 cat to get to the breaks."

"Mr. Rivera, I've driven cats all over the Interior," Laura said confidently. "You got a Hobart welding unit?" Again Rivera nodded. "There's nothing made out of metal I can't weld. I've welded cat tracks in 40 below weather. Aluminum skidder housing. Broken winch supports. Why, I've…"

Rivera laughed again. He sat back in his chair and waved his hands. "OK, OK. Enough." He chuckled. "Rusty was right. He said I'd hire you."

Laura sat back. She beamed from ear to ear.

Running the ranch was as hard as Rivera had warned. But it was work that Laura loved. Even though she cursed when the damned irrigation lines split. When she had to repair a broken chain on the swather. When the rain ruined a crop. Laura loved it. And she was good.

For five years she managed the entire operation. The book-keeping was the hardest. And she found the manuals harder and harder to read. But she had a small house. And Rachel seemed somewhat settled.

The five years hadn't been as easy for Rachel. She had trouble in school. Fought. Laura remembered her own school days. Rachel withdrew more and more into herself. Finally, when she was 15, Laura persuaded her to see a counsellor. Rachel had gone to her for more than a year. That had helped. Rachel had brightened.

But school was still a struggle. When she turned 16 she quit. Laura did all she could to convince her to stay. But it was useless.

Rachel began working at a convenience store and gas station. It wasn't a great job. But Rachel was bright. And she worked hard. She began to get promotions.

One afternoon she came home from work. She seemed gloomy. Laura began to worry. Rachel hadn't been depressed for over a year.

Laura poured two cups of coffee. She offered one to Rachel. Rachel took it without looking up. Laura sat in the rocker across from her.

"So how was your day?" Laura asked carefully.

"OK, I guess."

"Really?"

"Yeah. Riley stopped in. He's the district manager. He called me into the office in the back."

Oh, no, thought Laura. Had she been fired?

"He wanted me to manage the three stores in Ashcroft, Spences Bridge and Savona."

"But that's great!"

Rachel looked like she was going to cry. "There's one problem. I don't have my grade 12."

Laura sat back in the rocker. She rocked gently for a while.

"So what can you do?"

Rachel shrugged. "I'll never go back to school. I can't stand it." Her lips were pressed in a tight line. She shrugged again. "I guess I'm out of luck."

Laura stopped rocking. "Want an idea?"

Rachel looked up. "Sure."

"You know, my schooling was pretty awful too. Oh, I can read well enough to get by. But it's catching up with me. I can't read the manuals anymore. And the regulations! Cripes, they use words I've never even heard of. And now Ray wants me to get online with a computer. What do I know about computers?"

Rachel took a sip of her coffee. She looked at her mother. "So what are you going to do?"

"Well, I've been over to the college in Kamloops. They've got adult education classes there. All adults. I hung around and looked through the doors." Laura's eyes widened. "I couldn't believe it. The teachers talked to the students like they were adults. They talked to each other. It really is like college. So I spoke with a counsellor. I can probably get my grade 12 equivalent in a year."

Rachel smiled. "Mom, that's great! But what does that have to do with me?"

Laura leaned forward in the rocker. "Let's do it together."

14

Laura had worried about how Ray Rivera would respond. Would he say no? Maybe he'd fire her. But Laura was astonished by his reaction.

"Great! You know, I had thought about suggesting you get some upgrading. But I didn't want to insult you. And you're doing such a great job! I sure didn't want to lose you."

Fortunately, most of the classes were in the winter. Things were slower then. Ray made arrangements for his assistant manager to help Laura out while she was in school.

Rachel's boss was even happier. They gave her a year's leave of absence. And a guarantee of the management position when she was done.

School was both more challenging and more satisfying than Laura had expected. She had dreaded English when she had been a child. Laura had expected more of the same: adjectives, pronouns, verbs. She had convinced herself that she couldn't get it. But at college it was different. She was encouraged to write about her life. Her feelings and experiences. She kept a journal. She never thought she could put so many words together. But every night they tumbled onto the paper.

Laura enjoyed sharing her stories with other students. And she listened with respect and growing admiration. Students read about their lives, their struggles. Their hopes, their joys. And the teacher, as well as the other students, cared. There was gentle feedback from the instructor and students. Laura found her writing getting easier. Stronger. Clearer.

She had particularly dreaded reading. Laura had barely read a book in her life. But the books she was able to choose in class were different. They made sense. They were about people she cared about. About things she knew about. Sometimes they read and discussed articles from the local paper. She started slowly. But as she got more involved, the reading too came easier. Assignments were clear. She was given the skills to do them. Many of the writing assignments asked her what she thought. She was organizing her ideas, her opinions.

Math, too, had scared Laura. She struggled with fractions, equations. But the teacher was helpful. And Laura decided to treat it like a jigsaw puzzle. She patiently went at it piece by piece. And eventually it came together.

Rachel was a star. Her writing was read to the class. She helped other students with their math. She zipped through science labs. What had been so hard in the past now seemed easy.

And slowly the two women became even closer. They supported each other at home. Laura had to stretch to keep up with Rachel. Rachel read her mother's papers. Laura read Rachel's.

They did projects together. Rachel helped Laura with her math. They talked school at dinner. It spilled over into their chores. They found themselves arguing about things they had learned in social studies.

The days were full. Although she had help, Laura still had to maintain the farm. Rachel was always there with her. Laura felt a new kind of love for Rachel.

In May, Laura and Rachel's English teacher, Jason, asked to speak with them. They met him in his office. Laura poked her head through his open door. Jason's head was down. Piles of essays were at each elbow. Stacks of journals were heaped on the floor.

"Knock, knock," Laura said.

Jason looked up. He seemed a little dazed. "Oh, right. Laura. Rachel. Come in."

There was only one chair in the cramped office. Laura motioned to Rachel.

Rachel shook her head. "Please. Age before beauty."

Laura tried to sound severe. "I may be old, but I can still kick your butt. Now sit down."

"Oh, sorry," Jason said. "Wait a minute." He bustled out the door. In a few seconds he came back with a plastic chair. Laura took it and sat down.

"Listen, I…" Jason stopped. He looked a little sheepish. "I hope you won't be mad."

Laura looked puzzled. "Mad at what?"

"Well," Jason grimaced. "You know, I'm pretty proud of you two."

Laura was getting suspicious. "Thanks."

"And so, I…" He stopped. Then he finished in a rush. "I mentioned you to our publicity director. That you were graduating together. Mother and daughter, you know. And he called the radio. And, well, would you mind being interviewed on CBC tomorrow?"

"Huh?" Laura managed.

"Us?" Rachel asked.

"Yep. You two. It's not every day a mother and her daughter graduate together."

Laura felt her heart pound. She'd never been on radio, TV or anything else.

"I don't want to," she said.

Rachel grabbed her mother around the neck. She pretended she had her in a choke hold. "Come on, Mom. Anyone that can skid trees can talk on the radio."

"It's not the same at all. Out there it's just you and the skidder. But on the radio there will be thousands of people watching."

"Listening, actually," Jason corrected.

"That's kind of the idea, Mom," Rachel pointed out. She looked at Jason. "We'll do it."

Jason beamed. "You will?"

"We will?" Laura moaned.

Jason was clearly delighted. "OK. They'll call you at 9:00 tomorrow morning. Do you have two phones?"

Laura nodded miserably.

"Great. Have fun."

Laura didn't sleep at all that night. Her tossing disturbed Tiger on the end of her bed. He finally growled in irritation. Laura got up early in the morning. She fixed herself a pot of coffee. She worried about what they would ask. What if she made a fool of herself?

At 8:00 Rachel came down. "Sleep well?"

Laura glared at her.

"Oh, relax, Mom. It'll be fine. You'll see."

Just then the phone rang. They both jumped. Then they laughed. They continued laughing hysterically as the phone rang. Finally Laura picked it up. It was Clara.

"Rachel said you were going to be on the CBC. Just wanted to wish you luck. We're all tuned in here."

Laura hung up and had another cup of coffee.

The phone rang again at precisely 9:00. Laura's heart jumped into her mouth. She picked up the phone.

"Ms. Martin?"

"Yes."

"This is CBC radio."

Laura nodded to Rachel. She dashed to the phone in the kitchen.

Almost immediately the interviewer came on. "So today we are going to speak with two unusual graduates. A mother, Laura Martin, and her daughter, Rachel. Laura and Rachel, are you there?"

Laura couldn't speak. Finally she heard Rachel. She was cool, relaxed. "We're here. Good morning."

"I'm here too," Laura squeaked.

"Now Ms. Martin, Laura, that is. We understand you used to drive a skidder. Isn't that a little unusual for a woman?"

Laura was still nervous. But she had to snicker a little. "I'm an unusual woman."

The interviewer laughed. "Indeed you are. Now let's talk about your schooling."

Laura began to relax. She told about being at Willingdon. About having to work when she was young. Having to support a child. Rachel mentioned personal problems as the main reason she had left school. Then they chatted about the college. What they had enjoyed about it. How it had been different from their childhood school experience.

And it was just about over. Then Laura heard Rachel on the other line.

"Can I say one last thing?"

"Certainly. Go ahead."

"I just want to say that there isn't a better mother in the world than mine. She has always been there for me. I couldn't have done this without her. I couldn't have done a lot of things without her. We've become good friends going to school. But it's more than that too. I've grown to realize how much I love her. You're right. She is an unusual woman. She's had a tough life too. But she came through it. She's the strongest, kindest, most loving woman alive."

The announcer paused for a moment. "Thanks," he said. "Thanks to both of you. And congratulations."

Laura slowly hung up the receiver. She leaned back in the rocker she was sitting in. She fingered Blackie's locket. Old Tiger tried to climb into her lap. She helped him up. He purred loudly. Laura heard Rachel making breakfast in the kitchen.

And then the tears came. At first they trickled out like a few raindrops in the desert. But then it was like a dam inside had burst. Tears streamed down her cheeks like a river that had been blocked by ice. They trembled on her chin. They fell on Tiger's orange fur. Great sobs rose from within her. Laura cried.

Rachel rushed in from the kitchen. She ran to her mother. She took her hand anxiously.

"Mom. Mom, what is it? What's wrong?"

Laura smiled through the tears. "Nothing," she quavered. Her shoulders trembled. "Nothing at all." She gripped Rachel's hand hard. She looked into her daughter's face. "Everything's fine now."